T0107299

Lizard's Leap

Lizard's Leap

Kat Black

iUniverse, Inc.
New York   Bloomington

Lizards Leap

Copyright © 2009 by Kat Black

This is a work of fiction. All of the characters, names, incidents, organizations, and dialogue in this novel are either the products of the author's imagination or are used fictitiously.

iUniverse books may be ordered through booksellers or by contacting:

iUniverse
1663 Liberty Drive
Bloomington, IN 47403
www.iuniverse.com
1-800-Authors (1-800-288-4677)

Because of the dynamic nature of the Internet, any Web addresses or links contained in this book may have changed since publication and may no longer be valid. The views expressed in this work are solely those of the author and do not necessarily reflect the views of the publisher, and the publisher hereby disclaims any responsibility for them.

ISBN: 978-1-4401-2687-1 (pbk)
ISBN: 978-1-4401-2688-8 (ebk)

Printed in the United States of America

iUniverse rev. date: 2/11/2009

Chapter One
In The Beginning

An air of excitement popped along with the Rice Krispies at breakfast that morning. This was the long-awaited Saturday, which had captured Mark's imagination and creativity for weeks, the day of the school's summer fair. His sister, Vicki, was less impressed and enthusiastic. She felt that, at her age, she had outgrown extracurricular school events. Mark had been making and baking, collecting and selecting, painting and sticking and doing all manner of other fair-related activities. While his sister had moaned and groaned, sighed and ridiculed and generally been as unhelpful and teenage-girlish as possible. For once, the two dominating subjects of conversation were not fit lads and football but how much water should be added to icing sugar to make the cake frosting. The sunny, second Saturday in June had arrived, and they would be going with their mother to St Mary's Junior School Summer Fair. As far as Vicki was concerned it was just so un-kewl.

That morning, just like every other, Mark and Vicki Forest were arguing. Mrs Forest was busying herself with a batch of hot biscuits that she had just taken from the oven. The smell of the warm, fresh treats wafted out from the kitchen and spread throughout the house. It was tempting and delicious. It was also something of a rarity;

Mrs Forest was not given to home-made baking. She was especially not given to baking home-made goodies at nine-thirty on a Saturday morning when she could be having a lie-in. Mark and Vicki were allowed one each and munched happily. They sniggered behind their biscuits when their mother burned herself while taking a second batch out of the oven and swore. Like baking, Mrs. Forest was not given to swearing.

Victoria Anne Forest was the eldest of the four children. At thirteen years old, her greatest passion in life was boy bands. She knew everything there was to know about Get This, The Herb Boyz and countless others. Her bedroom walls were adorned with bright posters of her heroes, all with dazzling white teeth and big cheesy grins.

Nobody would ever have been unkind enough to call her daft, but ditzy and scatterbrained were two words that fit her as snugly as her low rise jeans. Vicki was a chatterbox. She always had a lot to say, and sometimes, some of it even made sense.

Mark Forest was Vicki's brother. He was nine.

Mark was clumsy. He regularly fell over his feet. He fell over other people's feet, and he even fell over invisible feet. He walked into things, dropped things, broke things, lost things, stood on things, forgot things, stubbed his toe, skinned his shin, banged his head, cut his hand, and grazed his knee... daily. Mark was a walking disaster, a public liability and a pest. He was also loud. Mark saw no sense in talking to somebody quietly. If he shouted, then he could reach a much wider audience and possibly annoy ten people instead of one. He called it, 'value for oxygen'.

"Mu-um," Vicki moaned, in her usual two-tone whine. "Mark said Luke Dross is rubbish, and that he's stupid."

"Did he, love?" sympathised Mrs Forest. "Well," she said, in mock seriousness, "he can't look good *and* be clever, now, can he?" Mrs Forest smiled to herself as she turned away from her daughter.

Mark was ecstatic with this minor triumph over his sister and wasted no time in beginning his victory chant. "Luke Dross is a moron. Luke Dross is a moron. And even Mum thinks so."

Vicki had heard quite enough. She jumped up from the table, preparing to stomp off in her best huffy manner. How dare they insult the Godlike Luke Dross?

"Er, just one minute, young lady. Where do you think you're going? I did not hear you excuse yourself from the table. And those dishes aren't going to rise up and float into the dishwasher by themselves, you know."

Vicki turned back to the table and sat down. "Sorry, mum. May I be excused, please?" She managed this with good grace so her mum nodded with a smile that she was allowed to leave the table. The children set about clearing the breakfast debris while bickering over whose iced buns were the most artistic.

In a similar kitchen three streets away, much the same morning rituals were taking place. This was the home of Emma and Kerry Taylor. Mrs Forest was Mr Taylor's sister. This made Vicki, Mark, Emma and Kerry, cousins. The four children were also best friends… Sometimes. Mrs Taylor was icing a huge chocolate cake. It looked almost too good to eat, but, given half the chance, neither Emma nor Kerry would care about that. The girls were very excited about the school fair and chatted ten to the dozen as they watched their mother. They repeated at five minute intervals that it was going to be a, boss rockin' day.

*

St Mary's summer fair was in full swing. The four cousins had opted to take the first turn on the stalls. Vicki no longer attended St Mary's, having moved the September before last to a secondary school, but she was still allowed to take a turn with Emma running the Tombola stall. It felt odd to be back at her old school and was a reminder that she was always getting into trouble when she had been a pupil at St Mary's. Like, for instance, the time when Miss Jameson had told her off for humming in the middle of a history lesson.

At playtime, Vicki had been talking to some of the girls. She had them all bent over laughing as she did an impression of Miss Jameson. Vicki said that her teacher, "had a face like a bulldog chewing a wasp." The girls had suddenly gone quiet. So, to try and get another laugh, Vicki just mentioned that the elderly teacher, "could do with a personality transplant." The girls looked at their feet and shuffled. Vicki didn't understand this so she tried another joke at the teacher's expense. "Miss Jameson is such an old bag that you could put your shopping in her," she had said loudly, before following the gaze of one of the girls and seeing none other than the dreaded Miss Jameson standing behind her. The two had never got along well after that, and Vicki always tried to keep a healthy distance from the teacher whenever possible.

Mark and Kerry had been in charge of the White Elephant stall. Mark was upset because in all the junk they had there was not one single white elephant. Well, to be more specific there had not been any elephants at all - white or otherwise. Kerry told him not to use the word, 'junk' in front of the customers. She used a little creativity and called the chipped ornaments and battered books, "finest antiques from the Jurassic era. Which means," she said, "junk from way back, when the dinosaurs still walked the earth."

Later, having finished their stints as stallholders, the children had been relieved of their duties and were now free to wander around and spend their pocket money.

"Oh look," said Vicki, pointing excitedly at the bric-a-brac stall. "It's a poster of The Big Wet Wusses. I have got to get it before Sharon Lazenby does, otherwise, she'll brag all next week. If I can get there first she'll be green with envy. And, anyway, I can brag better than she can, so I deserve to have it." With that, Vicki flew across the hall, dragging a surprised Kerry behind her. Emma and Mark rolled their eyes at each other and moved on to the cake stall, hoping to buy four of Mrs Forest's chocolate chip cookies if they hadn't sold out.

"I got it! I got it!" Vicki came charging back after just a couple of minutes. Her cheeks were slightly red with excitement, and her eyes shone. She waved the poster of the chart-topping boy band over her head.

But she was running too fast and crashed into Miss Jameson just as the class three teacher chose that precise moment to come around the corner. Vicki nearly bonked her on the head with the poster as she went past.

"Oops, sorry, Miss! Didn't see you there," muttered Vicki, colouring an even deeper red.

Mark sniggered into his hands. *Vicki's for it now*, he thought.

Miss Jameson looked as sour as usual, even amidst the excitement of the summer fair. "Victoria Forest. I see the new school has not begun to make a young lady of you yet. Please try not to do anybody any serious harm with that…that…what *is* that, anyway?"

"It's a poster of the Big Wet Wusses, Miss. They are at number one in the charts."

Miss Jameson took the poster from Vicki's hands. Vicki held her breath. What if the old battleaxe ripped it up? *I wouldn't put it past her*, she thought, praying silently that the precious, glossy picture of the five young men would survive the scrutiny.

Miss Jameson unrolled the poster slowly and deliberately. She looked at it for a long time. It showed Tommy Knocker, the lead singer, wearing no shirt, baring his entire chest. Vicki had a bad feeling about this. *If she doesn't rip it up, she's bound to confiscate it*, she thought as she began to hop from one foot to the other impatiently. *If she rips it, Sharon Lazenby will never believe that I ever had the poster!*

Vicki fretted as Miss Jameson peered at the picture of the young men. She finally finished looking at the poster over her half moon glasses. Rolling it back up with care, she did the most extraordinary thing any of them had ever seen her do. She began to sing in a very gruff voice that was very nearly, but not quite, in tune. This woman was no Tommy Knocker, but it was his number one song all right:

"If you're gonna hurt me, don't hurt me. Love me good - yeah baby,

If you're gonna love me, just love me. Don't cover me in mud - yeah baby."

Miss Jameson accompanied this rendition of 'Love Me' by bending her knees and wiggling her bottom. She moved her arms in front of her and looked like a bloated train chugging towards them. The four children were amazed and stared at the elderly teacher with open mouths. Miss Jameson winked at them, and said very formally, "Good day, children." She walked off.

The cousins looked at one other in astonishment. Suddenly, they all burst into gales of laughter. Miss Jameson, who was at the other side of the room by this time, must have heard them because she bent her knees and gave one more bottom-wiggle before disappearing out of the door. Vicki watched her former teacher leave with a very new level of respect for the lady, fancy her knowing the words to 'Love Me'.

The children wandered from stall to stall, haggling over trinkets and must-have articles that life simply couldn't continue without. They gorged on biscuits and joined their mothers, who were having coffee in the school's cafeteria. The children were given fizzy orange and, to Mark's delight, yet more biscuits.

Mrs Taylor was expecting a baby and looked very uncomfortable. The little one was due just before Christmas and would be a new brother or sister for Emma and Kerry. They both wanted it to be a boy and fought constantly over who would change his nappy and bathe him first. Mrs Taylor smiled at the thought of her sensitive children changing a soiled nappy.

Soon the cousins were bored with sitting at the table and listening to their mothers discuss what to prepare for the evening meal. They still had some money in their pockets that was screaming out at them, "Spend me! Spend me! Spend me!" Vicki and Mark had already parted with most of theirs, but Emma and Kerry had not spent much at all. This was the way it always was. On pocket money day Mark would go straight to the sweet shop to spend all of his money straight away. It was usually gone - with nothing to show for it - very quickly. Vicki was just as quick to spend hers, but it would go on posters and magazines. Emma would spend some of her money on one magazine or one packet of sweets and save the rest to use during the week. But Kerry would save all of her pocket money in her raptor moneybox, only taking it out when she had something really special to spend it on. That day she had grudgingly taken out two pounds, leaving her with thirty-six pounds eighty-seven pence.

The children were having a go on some of the side stalls. Emma won a bottle of apple and lemongrass bubble bath, and Mark won a knitted doll toilet roll holder that he was less than pleased about. Vicki was sulking because she only had about twenty pence left, and she hadn't won anything at all.

"Well, Vicki," said Emma, "It could be worse. You might have won that awful toilet roll holder that Mark got."

Now it was Mark's turn to sulk!

It was then that Kerry saw it. All day people had been coming with bags and boxes, stalls were constantly being added to as people donated their old 'what-nots', and stallholders would occasionally bring something up from the floor behind them. They had all been instructed to keep some of the better things back to add to the stalls as the day progressed. This meant that all the best items wouldn't be sold within the first five minutes, leaving nothing of interest for the rest of the day.

On the White Elephant stall Mrs Poole, the reception class teacher, had just finished sorting a box full of bits and pieces and arranging and displaying them to their best advantage. Kerry saw the picture of the Statue of Liberty from across the room, but it didn't interest her in the slightest. What did make her *need* that picture was the frame that housed it. It was beautiful! She made a beeline for the stall plucking up the tatty print as though it was a rare and undiscovered treasure.

Kerry was Emma's younger sister by two years. She was eight and younger than Mark by just a week -the baby of the four. Yet in some ways Kerry could be mistaken for the eldest. She was the most determined of the children and often got her own way. Once Kerry set her heart on something, she could be very determined.

The twelve-by-fourteen-inch frame looked very old. It had a broad section four-inches wide and was made from solid rosewood intricately carved with flowers and vines. But what made Kerry crave this item, what made her want it in a way that nothing else in the entire fair had inspired her, were the two carved lizards that climbed up the sides of the frame. The six-inch sand lizards were carved from the bulk of the wood. They were perfect in their detail and looked very realistic. Kerry ran her fingers over each of the lizards, lovingly. Like Vicki with the poster earlier, Kerry *had* to have this frame.

"Hello, Mrs Poole. How much is this picture, please?"

"Isn't it a beautiful picture, Kerry? It's the Statue of Liberty, you know. Let's see, now. How does two pounds grab you?"

Kerry's face fell. She looked down with something akin to loathing at the purchases she had already made - a stuffed rabbit with a loose eye, a game of Mastermind which may or may not have all the pieces intact and a book on ancient Egypt. She had been pleased with the book and was looking forward to reading it, but the other items had been bought just for the sake of having bought something. She neither liked nor wanted them, and now it seemed they would cost her the beautiful picture frame. Kerry reached into her purse and took out the remaining money. She had just eighty-two pence.

"Hey, Kerry!" Mark shouted, as he appeared at her side, startling her and almost making her drop the last of her money. "Wazz-up?"

"Oh, Mark, I'm glad to see you," Kerry said. "Have you got any money left?"

Mark looked at his cousin with suspicion. She had just said two very worrying things. The first was that she was glad to see him. People were not usually glad to see Mark, and if they were they *never* told him so. And secondly, she asked him if he had any money left. Now, Mark wasn't the brightest child in the entire solar system, but he knew that when Kerry asked if he had any money left it was going to mean trouble.

"Might have. Dunno."

"Well look, stupid," Kerry snapped at him.

"Oh well, if you're gonna start shoutin` at me I'm going to take my money and buy a cake or somefink."

Kerry knew better than to lose her temper and start shouting at him. It wouldn't do *any* good. So she set her features into what she hoped was her sweetest smile.

Mark checked his flies. He didn't like this game. He didn't understand the rules. Kerry was smiling at him. His flies weren't down so she wasn't smiling at him because she was going to tease him about that. She must be smiling at him because she wanted something. Mark was ready to say goodbye to the last of his pocket money. He knew it was no good trying to argue with Kerry. She was smarter and would just make him feel guilty until he handed it over anyway, so he might as well give up without a fight.

"I've got thirty-six pence left. I was saving it for when they sell off all the left-over cakes cheap at the end of the fair but you can have it if you like."

Kerry was not above using her determination to get her own way but she was also a child with a fair sense of justice. She knew that for Mark to give her the last of his money was a pretty big sacrifice.

"Oh, thank you, Mark. Tell you what, I'll swap you your thirty-six pence now for a pound when we get home."

Kerry now had one pound eighteen. She still clutched the picture possessively. Vicki and Emma had ambled over at some point throughout this exchange.

"How much do you need, Kez?" Vicki asked. "I've still got twenty pence that you can have as long as you give me it back later. There's nothing else I want here, anyway."

"Thanks, Vicki. That means I've got one pound thirty-eight pence. I'm still sixty-two pence short. Can you help me please, Emma?"

"Nope! No way," Emma had her 'I possibly *could* help, but don't see why I should' head on.

Emma was the eldest of the two sisters. She was ten and a very important three-quarters. It had to be said that Emma had *attitude*, and yet, almost in contradiction to this, she was a shy girl and the least self-assured of the four children. If somebody she did not feel comfortable with spoke to her, she hung her head and mumbled incoherently into her cardigan. But get the same girl on her own terms and she was a natural comedian. Emma was the one with the off-the-cuff, quick-as-a-flash, witty replies. She had an answer for everything and could be more sarcastic than most people three times her age. Emma was the clown of the four, always playing practical jokes on the others, and always looking for the funny side of any situation. She was also the one who could bear a grudge for all of eternity and then one week more.

"Oh, Emma, please. I'm desperate. I really, really want this frame. Please, Emma, don't be selfish."

"Well, I don't want to buy a share of a rotten old picture of the rotten old Statue of Liberty. And, anyway, last time I wanted to borrow ten pence off you, you said no. So now *I'm* saying NO. Tough talluda's baby."

This was very true. Kerry had not been keen to lend her sister some of her money. Now she felt sorry. Another point about Emma was her 'elephant' memory. They say an elephant never forgets. If somebody did something against Emma, she didn't forget it in a hurry. She had been sitting on this grievance for a long time, and this was her moment of glory.

"Maybe I will lend you the money, but it'll cost you."

Kerry was getting desperate. "Anything. Just tell me what you want."

"Five pounds, please." Emma stuck her chin out in a stance of defiance.

"Yo," Mark said, anticipating a fight. "Cool!"

"Aww! Emma, that's nasty. Don't be mean," Vicki cut in.

Kerry had a brainwave. "I'll tell you what. As I'm already giving Mark a pound, I'll give you and Vicki a pound each, too, providing you let me have the sixty-two pence. Please, Emma?"

"Deal!" Emma said emphatically. She wasn't a greedy girl. She had just wanted to teach Kerry a lesson.

Emma emptied her purse into her hand and began to count out the sixty-two pence. But Kerry's face fell when disaster struck. Emma only had fifty pence left. This meant that with all of them coppering up every penny they had, Kerry was still twelve pence short of being able to buy the beautiful carved frame. Their mothers had left some time ago, arranging to come back for the children later, so she couldn't ask them. There was nothing else to be done.

Kerry felt tears stinging her eyes as she placed the picture back on the front of the stall. She felt ridiculous, it was only a stupid picture so why did she feel strongly enough about it to almost be in tears at the thought of not having it? She shook her head, angry with herself for being so silly.   Mrs Poole came back over.   "Changed your mind, Kerry?"

"Yes, Miss."

"Oh, that's a shame.   It's a beautiful picture."

"Yes, Miss."

"Have you gone off it now?" she asked.

"No, Miss.   Haven't got enough money, Miss."

"O-oh, I see," said Mrs Poole.   "Well, how much have you got?"

"One pound eighty-eight, Miss."

"Well, you know, now that I look at it again, it does look a bit dirty.   I don't think it's worth two pounds, after all.   I think I'd be very pleased if I got one pound eighty-eight for it.   So it's yours if you want it, Kerry."

Kerry's face lit up like a tree at Christmas.   She was delighted and walked away with the picture in a large carrier bag.   She couldn't wait to get home and clean up the frame.   Her mind was racing with what she would actually put in it to replace the Statue of Liberty print that didn't do it justice.   She was ecstatic as she walked across the hall with the frame clutched tightly to her chest.

Suddenly, Kerry's step faltered and she stopped in the middle of the hall.   Standing by the door was a strange looking lady, and she was staring straight at Kerry.   The others had carried on walking and Kerry looked around to see if there was somebody else near her whom the lady could be looking at so intently.   But no, the woman was definitely looking at her.   She felt uncomfortable and a little scared.

The lady did look very odd.   She was quite old, sort of bent over, and yet at the same time there was something about her that didn't look old at all. She was a large lady, not very tall but quite round. Grey hair was pulled into a bun at the back of her neck and little wisps had come loose, falling over her face. She looked as though she had probably started the morning tidy and smart, but as the day had worn on she had begun to come apart a bit.

On the top of her head was a floppy black hat that looked too small for her. Perhaps it had slipped, or maybe she had put it on at an odd angle that made her look comical? Whatever the reason it did look funny. Her clothes were strange, too. She wore a purple skirt that had little silver bells around the bottom, and it was so long that it brushed the floor. The toes of scuffed, black boots just stuck out from underneath her skirt, and when she moved her foot Emma could see that they laced up the front like the old-fashioned boots that Victorian ladies wore. On her top half she had a long flowing tunic in purple and dark red, and around her neck was a bright orange silk scarf, which circled her throat several times and still trailed almost to her middle on both sides.

Kerry had never seen anybody who looked quite that colourful or mismatched before. What really caught her attention, though, were the lady's eyes. She stared straight at Kerry, and, as much as she wanted to, Kerry found that she could not look away. Those eyes fixed her with the most piercing stare that she had ever encountered. She looked down and her arms were covered in goose pimples. She shivered. The lady was scaring her.

Vicki came bounding back across the hall and linked

her arm though her cousin's. "Come on, slow-coach," she said. "What did you stop for?"

Kerry finally managed to break the stare with the strange lady. She turned to Vicki. "Vicki, look at that funny woman over by the door. She keeps staring at me."

"There's nobody by the door, stupid. Come on." With that she began to pull Kerry across the room.

Kerry looked back towards the door. The lady had gone!

They went outside to wait for their mothers. The women would be here to pick them up any time now so they walked around the corner and sat on a wall to wait. Kerry told the others about the strange lady. When she told them about the bright clothes and floppy hat, Mark and Emma laughed, but Vicki didn't.

"Oh, you're such a liar, Kerry. I think you're just making it all up. I looked in the hall and nobody was there."

"I am not making it up!" Kerry said indignantly. "She was there and she was a witch." This time they all started laughing, but Mark stopped very suddenly.

"Oh-oh," he said. "Here comes trouble."

The lady who had scared Kerry was walking towards them. They all recognised her from the description Kerry had given. It was her, alright.

"Flippin` heck," said Emma under her breath. "The sights you see when you haven't got a gun!" She had heard her dad utter this little gem when a middle-aged, scantily dressed lady had crossed the road in front of the car, just last week. Emma thought it sounded cool so she had stored it in her mind to bring out and use at just such an appropriate moment as this. Mark sniggered.

"See, Vicki," Kerry whispered. "I was *not* lying."

Vicki began to hum nervously. One of her most annoying habits was her singing. Vicki sung! That doesn't mean that Vicki *could* sing, although undoubtedly she could. It meant that Vicki *did* sing. She sang at breakfast and her mum told her off for singing at the table. She sang in class and Mrs Barnes told her off for being disruptive. She even sang on the bus until her dad shook his head and hid his face in his hands. Yes, Vicki sang... and hummed and clicked and sometimes just did, "la la la…"

The lady was out of breath by the time she drew level with the children. Her face was red, and she had a thin coating of perspiration on her forehead. Vicki instantly felt sorry for her. The strange lady walked slowly and with a slight limp. She had a wide bottom that swayed from side to side as she walked. The beads on her skirt jingled like tiny bells and the tiny bells kept time with the beads. She had a smile on her face and didn't look scary, but she was definitely coming over to them. Kerry began to rock backwards and forwards in time to Vicki's humming. Mark and Emma just stared at the approaching woman.

"Hello, my dears," the lady said, as she drew close to them. She was smiling broadly and Vicki thought she looked rather kind. "I'm sorry to bother you on this lovely sunny day. My name is Sylvia, and I just had to come and talk to you. You see, the picture that you have belongs to me, my lovelies. It was given to the fair by mistake and it holds great sentimental value, though it isn't worth much in actual money. Please, will you sell it back to me? You seem like such nice children and I'm sure you'll want to help a silly old woman. What are you all called?"

They were struck by the look on the lady's face. She had the greenest eyes any of them had ever seen. They were piercing and bright and so, so… green. Her body looked old, but her eyes made her appear to be a lot younger than she probably was. The lady was still smiling sweetly but somehow the smile never made it all the way up to her eyes. All four of the children felt a little nervous.

They looked at each other uncomfortably, not knowing what to do or say. None of them told the lady their names. Mark started kicking some stones with his shoes.

"I don't know nuffink about no picture," he lied, both unconvincingly and ungrammatically. The others looked at Kerry, who clutched the picture more tightly to her chest.

"I'm really very sorry," Kerry said politely, "but the picture isn't for sale."

The Lady smiled pleasantly at Kerry. "Oh, come on, now. What can you possibly want with it? It's only a foisty old picture. How much did you pay for it? I'll give you double."

Kerry was starting to feel a little scared. She looked at the ground and muttered in a very small voice, "I don't want to sell it. Sorry."

"Little girl, I need that picture back." The old lady suddenly wasn't quite so nice. She wasn't nasty exactly, but the friendly tone had disappeared out of her voice, and the smile had faded. "I'll give you five pounds for it."

Kerry shook her head stubbornly.

"Ten," the lady said icily, her gaze boring into the top of Kerry's lowered head.

Again Kerry shook her head. She felt tears stinging her eyes. The lady was scaring her, but for some reason that she didn't understand Kerry knew the picture was very important to her, even though she had only owned it for just fifteen minutes. She couldn't let it go now. Like the lady said, it was only a picture, and yet she felt more attached to it than anything else she owned. It didn't make sense.

Vicki risked looking up at the woman. She had been told many times not to talk to strangers. They all had. She looked past the lady and back towards school. Maybe they should go back inside and let a teacher sort it out, but that would mean pushing past the lady.

"I would like you to give back my picture *now*, please, young lady. Or I will ring your parents and sort it out with them. I haven't got time to be standing here arguing. Now, give me the picture, please."

She took a step towards Kerry and held out her hand for the picture.

"Go away, please, or we'll call a policeman," shouted Emma. She looked frantically round for a grown-up to call out to.

It was all too much for Mark. "RUN!" he shouted, and the next thing anybody knew he was off down the road as fast as his legs could carry him. Almost as a reflex reaction the others followed him, their feet pounded the road as they ran full pelt down the hill.

"Steady on, legs," said Emma, in her deep voice, as her legs seemed to be going faster than her body could keep up with. They ran round a corner and leaned against the wall panting.

"Where's Vicki?" they all shouted in unison.

"Oh, no, the Wicked Witch of the North has got her," said Emma.

Vicki had made a run for it with the others, but she had been just a fraction of a second slower to catch on. The lady made a grab for her. She caught Vicki by the upper arm and gripped her painfully. Vicki cried out and looked at the woman, terrified. The lady's green eyes seemed to be even brighter than they had been a few minutes earlier. They flashed with anger and impatience. Vicki found that she couldn't look away from them.

"Don't be silly, child," said Sylvia. "I'm not going to hurt you. You are all being foolish. You should have given the frame back to me. You don't know what you have or what you are dealing with. I have to warn you to be careful. You could be in terrible danger if you are not very careful."

Vicki was scared out of her wits by this time. She twisted out of the crazy woman's grip and stumbled to the ground, grazing her knee. She was free and began to limp off towards the others with tears streaming down her cheeks and blood trickling down her leg. She heard the old woman calling after her, "I'm Sylvia Sanders, child! I live in Brampton Hall! Come to me when you need my help! Beware of the picture! You don't know what you're dealing with!"

*

The children ran all the way to Emma and Kerry's house, which was the closest to the school. They burst through the door just as their mother was leaving to pick them up. Through tears and much excited babble the children recounted their story. Vicki felt very important as she showed her mother the ugly bruise on her upper arm. Karen Forest and Debbie Taylor were furious. You heard of people approaching children at schools all the time, but never expected it to happen to *your* children. They rang the school to make a formal complaint. Then they rang the police. The policeman who came out to interview the children listened to their story, making notes in his book and stopping them every now and then to ask the occasional question.

"Are you sure the lady said Brampton Hall, Vicki?" the officer asked her.

"Yes. Positive."

"Well, that's funny," said the Policeman. "Brampton Hall has been empty and shuttered up for years." He left with a promise to look into the incident.

Later, at Granddad's house, the children were in Kerry and Mark's room. They had the frame on the bed in front of them, but no matter how closely they looked, they couldn't see anything special about the twelve-by-fourteen-inch picture.

"Scary!" said Mark.

"As Scooby-Doo," replied Emma, and they laughed for the first time since getting away from the creepy woman. Mrs. Taylor said they should feel sorry for the strange lady because she obviously had some mental problems.

"Yes, she's nuts!" Emma said, with her usual comic timing.

But that night both sets of children slept with the lights on and their bedroom doors open.

Chapter Two
Liberty Island

Sunday morning squeezed itself through the chink in the dinosaur curtains. It landed squarely on Mark and Kerry's bedroom carpet, waking Kerry up and demanding an early start to the new day. She knew it was Sunday because she could hear the church bells calling the faithful to worship. She loved Sundays; they were different from any other day and had a special feel about them. However, the other sound in the room was not nearly as pleasant as that of the church bells. Mark was snoring softly to himself in the other bed. Kerry remembered that they had all stayed the night at their nanna and grandad's house.

The Taylors and the Forests were an extended-but-close family. The two mothers were not only sisters-in-law but also best friends and the children had all been brought up together. The hub of the family was the big house on the hill where the children's grandparents lived. All the family gatherings occurred there. Normally, at the weekend, the four children stayed at their nanna and granddad's, going back home after tea on Sunday. They had their own bedrooms. Mark and Kerry shared one room because they were the youngest, and Vicki and Emma shared the other. They always had a lot of fun at their grandparents' house and were having a big family meal later that day. Suddenly, the day before came flooding back to Kerry, and she shivered as she remembered the creepy woman and her crazy warning.

Kerry was a girl of unusual interests. She was fascinated almost to the point of obsession by dinosaurs, reptiles, and fossils. She soaked up any morsel of information on her pet subjects and stored it in her mind to mull over and play with later. She would sit for hours reading and learning all about the things that interested her. Kerry was going to be a scientist, a palaeontologist, in fact, which meant that she wanted to study dinosaurs and fossils and primitive man. But Kerry said that she wasn't sexist so she was going to study primitive lady, too. She was only eight and could spell palaeontologist without looking it up in a dictionary. The other three children were envious of this ability, and, although they teased her about it, secretly they would all have liked to be able to do it too. The other big love in Kerry's life was ballet. She went to lessons every week, and practiced daily. One day Kerry aimed to write her own ballet. She was going to call it "Dinosaur Valley".

She looked across the room at the cast iron fireplace. These days it was just kept for ornamental value as no fire had been lit in it for years. Instead, the hearth was filled with a cascading dried flower arrangement. But this morning it had a new decoration. The precious wooden frame sat on the mantelpiece and set off the fireplace to stunning effect. All it needed was a suitable picture to replace that awful Statue of Liberty print. Kerry couldn't wait to give it a good clean. She hoped that maybe there would be something of the right size and suitability in the house to grace the carved frame. If not, she was prepared to wait until she could find *just* the right picture.

At the weekend, breakfast wasn't put on the table until about half past nine. It was a Sunday tradition that the family sat down to a large cooked breakfast. This made Sunday Mark's favourite day, a big breakfast, followed by buffet style lunch, and a huge roast dinner in the evening. He looked forward to Sundays above all other days. It was a day of almost unlimited eating. Breakfast consisted of cereal or porridge, followed by bacon, eggs, sausage, tomatoes, mushrooms and fried bread. They always sat around the breakfast table for a long time. Kerry talked constantly about the picture frame until the others got fed up hearing about it. After breakfast the children watched a film, but Kerry's mind was on the picture, and she couldn't concentrate on High School Musical II, at all. Kerry tended to be a bit obsessive about things and when she had something on her mind there was no room in there for anything else. As soon as the film came to an end, she jumped up, anxious to get upstairs to clean her picture frame. She would just about have time to finish it before lunch at twelve thirty.

Kerry borrowed a soft duster, some polish, and wax from her nanna. She couldn't wait to make a start on cleaning the frame.

Vicki knocked on the bedroom door and wandered in. "Do you want to listen to my new 'Live Lounge' CD, Kez?" Without waiting for an answer, she put the CD in the compact music centre and turned up the volume.

"Turn that music down right now!" Nanna's voice floated up the stairs. Vicki pulled a face and reluctantly turned the music down, but not very much.

Kerry was sitting cross-legged on the floor, turning the frame over and over in her hands, feeling the grain. She enjoyed the smooth finish of the wood and the knobbly contrast when her fingers ran over the lizards. She had neither looked up nor spoken since Vicki had entered the room. Vicki was used to this. Kerry often absorbed herself in what she was doing to the point that she became unaware of things taking place around her. It didn't bother Vicki. She chattered away in a lively one-way conversation, seeming not to notice that she was actually talking to herself. She lounged back on Kerry's bed and broke off her string of chatter with the odd blast of singing along with the songs on the CD. Kerry rocked slowly backwards and forwards, enjoying the moment when she would begin to actually clean the frame and let the dirt-hidden beauty of the wood shine through as the muck was removed.

Emma knocked on the door and wandered in. "Kerry, may I borrow your *Ghost Stories* book, please?" She got no response, so shouted loudly, "Kerry! Can I borrow your book, please?"

"What?" said Kerry, shaken from her daydream. She looked at Emma as though she had no idea who she was. "Oh, yes, okay. It's on the bookcase. Make sure you put it back in the right place when you've finished with it, please. All my books are logged alphabetically and if it's not put back properly I'll know about it and I'll never lend anything to you again." With that she turned back to the picture.

Now at this point, Mark was still sitting in front of the television downstairs. He was playing with a plastic figure from the box of Coco-Pops that had caused a huge argument that morning. Nanna had finally stepped in and decreed that it was Mark's turn to have the gift. Still basking in his moment of glory, he heard the heavy bass beat of the dance music coming from upstairs. Looking around, he realised for the first time that he was alone and several thoughts tried to form themselves in some sort of order in his mind. The first of these was, "I wonder what they are doing up there?" Closely followed by, "They had better not be messing with my stuff!" Then, "I bet they're only talking about boybands and kissing," and, "But what if they are doing something interesting? Or, what if they have some sweets stashed that they don't want me to know about?"

With that last thought, Mark shot up off the chair and pounded up the stairs.

Bursting through the door, out of breath and panting, he was disappointed to find that Kerry was looking at that dumb old picture frame, and Vicki and Emma were sitting on Kerry's bed singing along to the music. He shuffled over to his bed and flopped down onto it.

"I'm bored!" This was Mark's second most often used phrase, the other being: "I'm hungry!" Nobody answered him.

Mark was a pain, and *his* greatest passion in life was to wind up his sister and their two cousins. Mark's other great love was food, and he was of the opinion that life should be a perpetual running buffet. He thought he might like to be the Prime Minister one day, and, when he was, all sweet shops would have to give their sweets to boys for free. But not to girls, Mark thought they were a different species and should have to pay extra - *and* get a smaller share, to boot. Mark didn't think much of boy bands, but he liked computer games and fighting with his sister.

Kerry squirted some furniture polish onto the top left-hand corner of the frame. She breathed in the smell of the polish and loved the woody aroma that was so familiar to her. She took the duster and wrapped it around one of her fingers. Slowly and methodically she began to rub the wood with tiny little circling movements. Her dad had taught her to clean her school shoes in this way with shoe polish. He told her that it's the way the soldiers do their boots in the army. They call it, bulling them. Only, her dad said that the soldiers often use spit to wet the polish and Kerry thought spitting was *disgusting. Her* shoes always seemed to come up bright and shiny without having to spit on them. She had already decided that she would never marry a soldier because they have some horrible habits. Adding more polish as was necessary, she continued working her way down the left-hand side of the frame and then along the bottom.

At the centre point of the bottom edge, her fingers found a small irregularity in the wood. She turned the frame over and noticed, for the first time, that hidden at the back of the edge was a three-inch long notch in the wood. Her fingers probed the opening.

Suddenly, she pulled her hands back with a gasp.

Something was moving!

Shocked, Kerry watched as a small drawer dropped from the bottom of the frame. "Wow! Come and look at this, you lot."

Already alerted by Kerry's surprised gasp, the other three had jumped off their beds and were crowding around Kerry on the floor. They stared at the little drawer.

"Look," Vicki said, stating the obvious. "There's something inside."

Kerry's fingers trembled slightly as she lifted a tiny, rolled tube of yellowed paper from the small drawer. It appeared to be very old. Vicki took it from her and opened it with extreme care, not wanting to rip the fragile paper. The old-fashioned writing was difficult to understand, but Vicki managed to read it out loud, deciphering the words as she went:

Here is an image for you to keep -
Follow where the lizards leap.
Move with caution, take a peep,
Beware! Do not get in too deep.

Repeat the words inscribed below;
Take a breath and off you go.

Sand Lizard, Sand Lizard, cautiously creep.
Shim. Sham. Shally wham. Lizards leap!

As Vicki read the last word the room began to spin. It moved slowly at first. Then it rotated faster and faster. It plucked them up from the bedroom and spun them around and round gaining speed like a spin dryer until the children found themselves inside a lightning-fast vortex, a tumbling, spinning world similar to the centre of a tornado. They spun and spun, unable to get enough breath to scream, unable to *think*, let alone have the time to be scared...

Then, as suddenly as it had begun to revolve, the vortex world slowed and came to a stop. The children found themselves sitting on a grassy area facing the sea. The bedroom had vanished. Across the water were a million twinkling lights, all attached to huge buildings. It was either very early in the morning or about ten o'clock at night, as it wasn't very light. Vicki looked at her watch. It should have said about quarter to twelve, but it actually said twenty to seven.

Before them was a long walkway leading to a circular paved area surrounded by railings. Beyond that, the sea hit the lookout wall spraying water up in sloshing waves.

The children looked at each other in astonishment. *Now* they had time to be scared and were taking full advantage of the fact. Vicki was the first to speak.

"Wha …what happened? Where *are we*?" Her voice rose on the second question until it became a wail.

"I don't know, Vix," Kerry said. "But at least *you've* got your clothes on."

Kerry looked down at herself. All the others had washed and dressed before breakfast, but Kerry, anxious to get breakfast over with quickly so that she could get back to the frame, had not bothered. Then she had been side-tracked by watching the movie, and somehow, she had just never got around to getting washed and dressed. She was still in her thin blue striped nightie. She pulled it down over her knees and shivered. She had on no socks or shoes, and the grass under her bare feet was cold and damp. She began to cry. "I'm scared," she sobbed. "Where are we? I want to go home."

Mark was the first to recover his composure. As the girls huddled together he stood up and turned in a slow, full circle. His eyes shimmered with unshed tears.

"Woooooow!" he breathed. "Don't look behind you girls, but we've got company. This is an amazing dream!"

The girls all snapped their heads round simultaneously. Standing behind them, gazing patriotically out to sea, the Statue of Liberty stood resplendent in her long copper dress. The children had to tilt their heads right back to be able to see the entire statue because it was so tall. Over the years the metal had become green and mottled, giving her the appearance of being a very old lady, though her face was smooth and finely sculptured. Her right arm was extended, and the torch that she held threw a beacon of light over the entire harbour. Her other hand held a thick book. The statue was breathtaking in its size and meticulous detail. The children were lost for words, in awe of this geographical sight.

Vicki wiped her eyes, a little of the fear leaving her as the wonder of the situation tried desperately to sink in. "It's the Statue of Liberty. I think, somehow, we've fallen into the picture. Mark's right, it must be a dream. I just wish it was *his* dream and not mine." Her voice wavered again and Kerry put her arm around Vicki's shoulders. Vicki looked at her watch, trying to make sense of what was happening to them. It should have said twenty to twelve, but *still* said it was twenty to seven. She shook her head, unable to understand what had just happened. Her watch wasn't giving away any clues.

"This is an island," said Emma. "The only way to get to the mainland is by boat. I remember reading about it once."

Kerry sniffled and then brightened as one of her 'interesting facts' came to her. "Do you realise," she said, to nobody in particular, "that if we were basilisk lizards, we could just rise up onto our back legs and walk over the sea. Basilisks are so light and so fast that they can skim over water without sinking."

"And if I was Jesus, I could walk over the water, too. But as I'm not, that isn't much help, is it, Kerry?" Emma snapped, sarcastically.

"Awwww, Emma," said Mark, obviously impressed. "You said a swear word."

"No I didn't. I meant Jesus the saviour, not Jesus the swear word. He's someone *completely* different."

"I've gone stark raving mad", Emma said, turning to the others. "Am I dribbling? Mad people always dribble."

"No more than usual," Mark said. "You've been mad for years."

"Pack it in, you two!" snapped Vicki. "We've got to work out how to get home from here. Do you think we really *are* in America? That's a long way from England." The enormity of that statement hit each one of the four children in turn.

Kerry, who had almost stopped crying, began to wail. "I want my mum," she sobbed, rocking furiously backwards and forwards. Vicki started to hum as she thought through their predicament.

"Maybe we'll be stuck here forever," said Mark, sadly.

"Don't be stupid," Emma replied. "This is the Statue of Liberty, dumbo. Lots of people come to see it. I think they might just notice us sitting here, eventually, don't you?"

"Do you think they'll send us home, Em, or put us in prison for coming into America without our passports?"

"I dunno, Vicki. What are you asking me for? Do you think I read a book on falling into pictures before we came, or something? Let's have a look around and see if we can find somebody to help us."

"Mark, take your fleece off and give it to Kerry," Vicki said.

"Huh, why me? You take *your* jumper off and give it to her."

"Mark, my dear brother, I have got nothing on under my jumper and I have nearly got bosoms. You have got a T-shirt on and will never have bosoms. Now, take your fleece off and give it to Kerry, please."

The girls laughed at this remark, and Mark graciously gave his warm fleece to a very grateful Kerry.

They stood up and looked across at what they guessed to be the part of New York called, Manhattan. It was spectacular in the partial darkness. They turned and walked along the sweeping walkway towards a group of buildings up ahead. The statue in front of them was magnificent. Her torch - so far above - burned brightly and seven rays of light shone across the water from the windows in her crown. The beams fell in strips along the dark waves of the harbour, and as they lapped gently towards Liberty Island the reflections of light danced on the sea's surface.

"I wish we'd brought a camera," said Vicki. "Sharon Lazenby is not going to believe *this*."

The walkway soon opened up onto a large courtyard. They wandered round the various buildings. There was a museum, public toilets, a cafeteria, a gift shop, and the railings, which were the queuing area for the statue itself. Everything was closed and unmanned. Mark moaned about being hungry, and Kerry moaned about her feet being cold and sore. They all moaned about their predicament, and yet, they were also, in a strange way, excited by this amazing adventure.

The children were relieved to notice that it was gradually getting lighter. It would have been awful to be stuck there all night. They comforted themselves with the fact that soon the first ferry would be coming across the water. They would be rescued. Somehow though, they doubted that their story would be believed.

Mark ran along the queuing gates until he found the door that led into the actual statue. He tried the handle but it was securely locked. Running his hand reverently over the smooth stone of the statue's plinth at the side of the door, he said, "I can't believe that I am really in the United States of America, and that I'm touching the famous Statue of Liberty. Isn't it amazing?"

They all touched the statue, just so that they could say they had. But who would ever believe them? They sat in the shelter of the doorway and pondered their plight, waiting for the first ferry to arrive.

"What time is it, Vicki?" Emma asked.

"Well, we left home at just after half eleven, so it must be about half past twelve now. The odd thing is that my watch says it's twenty five past seven."

"If it's lunch time, then how come it's so dark?" Mark puzzled.

"We-ell," Emma had been thinking this very problem through. "New York is five hours behind us in England. So-o, if it's half past twelve in England, it's still only half past seven in the morning in America. I think that's why it's only just got really light here."

"What time is it *really?*" asked Kerry. "Because if it's really seven thirty then we won't have been missed yet, but if it's really twelve thirty then Nanna will have realised by now that we are not in our room. She'll be so worried, and we'll be in so much trouble when she finds out we went to America without telling anyone." Kerry began to cry again with this new thought.

"But it isn't our fault, is it? We didn't *ask* to come to the rotten old Statue of Liberty when the café is closed," Mark reasoned.

Kerry took comfort from facts. It was one of her things and reciting facts was something she did when the world got too much for her. She knew a lot of facts. Most of them disjointed pieces of information learned from books and school lessons, or from documentaries on the television. "Do you know..." she began. The others groaned. "Do you know, that there are three hundred and fifty-four steps up to Liberty's crown, and that the twenty-five windows represent the twenty-five gemstones of the Earth? Or that the seven rays in the crown represent the seven seas and continents of the world?"

They were stunned into silence for a second by this impromptu lesson. It never failed to amaze the others that Kerry could rattle off so much information on so many diverse topics. They envied her.

"Oh, shut up, Kerry", they all said, unkindly, and in unison.

"And another thing," Kerry was on a roll and wasn't about to be swayed by their lack of appreciation. "If we managed to fall into a picture to get here, why can't we just fall out again to get back home?"

There was a long silence as this thought settled on

each of the four children. It *was* logical. If they had managed to just fall here, then surely, they should be able to just fall *back* again?

"Kerry, you are a genius," Vicki said, kissing her cousin firmly on the cheek. "There must be a way back through the picture. We just have to work out, how."

Emma remembered the piece of paper. "Vicki, it must have something to do with that weird poem you read out. What happened to the piece of paper that it was written on?"

"I don't know, do I? When the room started spinning, I must have dropped it on the carpet." She looked forlornly down at her hands as if she expected the piece of paper to magically appear.

For over half an hour they sat and desperately tried to remember what was written on the paper. It was hopeless. They tried so many different things, but none of them worked.

"Oh well," Mark said, cheerfully. "We're just going to have to go back to plan A, and wait to be rescued."

Kerry wailed.

The sun was fully risen by this time. Its rays shone down strong and bright, even though it was not yet nine o'clock in the morning American time. Kerry stretched her cold legs out to be warmed. Her face tilted upwards, and the sun worked hard to dry her tears as they fell. It didn't succeed and they continued to fall in fat splashes onto her legs.

"Look! Look!" Mark said excitedly. At the other side of the harbour a ferry was just leaving the jetty. Help was on its way. The children ran to the railings to meet it when it arrived. Kerry tried to hide behind the others.

She felt ridiculous, standing in broad daylight in her nightie.

The ferry was a two-tiered boat. It was covered on the lower deck and open on the top deck. The children could see people sitting on the bench seats inside the bottom tier. B*ut*! What made them draw back into the shadows of the plinth - so that they wouldn't be seen - was the figure standing alone, leaning on the top deck railings at the front of the ferry. The strong wind blew her grey hair back from her face, straggling wisps that stuck straight out of the back of her head like a flag. She held onto her floppy black hat with one hand and seemed to be fighting against the wind to keep her balance. She wore a bright green skirt, a vivid canary-yellow top and a scarlet scarf. The cousins knew of only one person who would dress like that.

"Sylvia!" they all said in unison.

The children shrank back against the plinth of the statue. It was too late. She had already seen them. She waved her arm and shouted but her words were taken by the wind and carried away on the waves. They could not make out what she said. They were trapped.

"Oh, great," Emma said. "Just when things were getting better, we have to run into a colour-blind crazy woman."

"How did she get here?"

"Did she know we would be here?"

"What will she do to us?"

"What if she goes mad and kills us all when she sees that we haven't got the picture with us?"

"What are we going to do?"

"What if the people on the ferry are all crazy?"

"How will anyone know we are here?"

"What if she eats children? Oh, I do hope she's a vegetarian."

These were all questions that the cousins threw at each other. Nobody had any of the answers. They huddled together, terrified.

They were all worried about whether they were going to get into terrible trouble. Now, they were also scared because Sylvia was getting nearer and they already knew she was crazy. Vicki rubbed her arm that bore the bruises from the day before. She looked at her watch. It was twenty five past eight Liberty time. Would Nanna have called the police by now?

Vicki stuck her hands in her pockets and began to sing quietly to herself. Her fingers touched something right at the bottom of her jeans pocket. She pulled it out and looked at it. Then she shrieked in excitement as she realised that it was the piece of paper from out of the frame. She hadn't dropped it on the bedroom carpet, after all.

"Quick! Quick!" the others shouted.

"Read the poem!" Kerry said urgently. "Come on, hurry, before she gets here!"

The ferry was just coming in to berth by the jetty.

With trembling fingers and stammering voice Vicki began to read, slowly at first, then faster as the words became more familiar to her.

Here is an image for you to keep -
Follow where the lizards leap.
Move with caution, take a peep,
Beware! Do not get in too deep.

Repeat the words inscribed below;
Take a breath and off you go.

Sand Lizard, Sand Lizard, cautiously creep.
Shim. Sham. Shally wham. Lizards leap!

The landscape around them began to move.

"Hooray!" cried Emma.

Mark stepped out from the shadows and, cheekily raising his arm, he waved at Sylvia. "Adios, amigos!"

Vicki grabbed his shirt and dragged him firmly back so that he wouldn't get left behind.

The world began to spin. Faster and faster it revolved. They were once again caught in the vortex. When it suddenly stopped spinning the four children were sitting on the floor in their bedroom, gazing at the picture of the Statue of Liberty.

"Whoa, cool!" said Mark. "That was awesome."

"Well, I suppose we had better go and face the music. All we can do is just tell the police the truth," Vicki said miserably.

At that moment there was a knock on the door, and Nanna stood there with the vacuum cleaner in her hand.

"I thought I asked you to turn that music down," she said, glaring at Vicki. "And as for you, Madam," she turned her attention to Kerry. "Do you ever intend to get dressed today, or are we having a pyjama party?"

Kerry ran over to her nanna and flung her arms around her waist. She buried her head in her grandmother's pinny, and smelled the familiar aroma of cooking and soap that *was* her nanna. "I do love you, Nanna," she said.

Vicki noticed for the first time that the same CD was playing as when they had left, although it was running a different track. She looked at her watch. It said twenty to nine. She looked at the clock on the wall in her bedroom. That one said ten to twelve. According to the bedroom clock they had only been gone ten minutes, and yet they had been away almost exactly two hours. That was impossible. She sat back on her heels to think it through.

"When you are in the picture, time moves normally, and yet here it slows right down. One hour is equal to five minutes," she mused.

"What a lovely lyric, dear. Who sings it?" her nanna asked, distractedly, already turning and halfway out of the door.

The cousins sat looking at each other, each of them lost in their own thoughts and impressions of their adventure.

"I wonder what would happen if we changed the picture in the frame?" Emma finally said.

Mark was the first one to ask what all four of them were thinking. "Well, when are we going to try it?"

Chapter Three
Shoo Fly.

The four children were in the middle of a very heated argument.

"Ah, but," Vicki said angrily, "you didn't pay us when you said you would."

"Exactly. That is why I am trying to pay you now," reasoned Kerry.

"It's too late now, Kerry. You should have paid us when you said you would. Now the frame belongs to *all* of us equally," Emma said.

"It's *my* frame, I tell you. *I* saw it. *I* bought it. It's mine and I'm not sharing it!" Tears stung Kerry's eyes, and she stamped her foot on the last word.

Vicki saw how upset her cousin was and her attitude softened. "Kerry, it's still yours, of course it is, and we know how special it is to you, but now it's special to the rest of us, too. We're all equally involved in the magic of the frame, and it's too big a responsibility for you to have on your own. I really think it would be better if you shared it with us." Vicki was now all done being understanding. "And, anyway, it already *does* belong to all of us because we all paid for it, and if you keep making a fuss I'll come over there and deck you."

"Yeeess," said Mark. "Go on, Vic. Bop her one."

"All right, then," Kerry moaned. "I'll share it. But you had better not do anything to damage it or ruin the magic because if you do I'll put slugs in your bed."

Vicki and Kerry glared at each other.

"It's staying in our room though, isn't it, Mark?" Kerry looked to her cousin for support.

Now, Mark knew how ugly these scenes between Vicki and Kerry could become and wasn't at all convinced that he wanted to be dragged into the middle of it. He looked shiftily between the two bristling girls, then back to Vicki. She didn't *look* as though she was going to run over and give him a Chinese burn, but you never could tell with Vicki.

"I dunno," he muttered.

"Agreed, then," Vicki said. "We are all equal joint owners, but it stays in your room."

"Slug slime becomes you, it goes with your hair," sang Emma, sensing that the war was over. They all started laughing, even Kerry, who still clutched the frame possessively.

She admired their new picture. She sat looking at it and went off into a daydream, reliving how they'd bought it the night before. None of the others paid any attention to her; they were used to her drifting off.

The evening before, their mum had taken her and Emma to an auction of household goods. They were there to see if they could find a suitable picture to fit the frame. This was the second week that they had been and Kerry was becoming impatient. The previous week there had been nothing but a load of old junk in Kerry's opinion. She was hoping that this week would be more successful.

Before the auction had begun they walked around viewing the lots. Emma was looking at ornaments for her room, but Kerry went straight over to where the pictures stood. She immediately saw one that she thought would look very nice. Emma came over and they huddled together discussing the suitability of this picture for "leaping". The view depicted would make a wonderful place to leap. Kerry solemnly got out her tape measure and measured the picture. It was fourteen-by-eighteen-inches and was a little bit too big, but that didn't matter. She could cut off some of the scenery around the edge to make it fit. The frame housing the picture was awful and didn't do it justice at all. It was a thick gilt frame and the gold coloured paint was gaudy and chipped. The print would look much better in the lizard frame.

The auction began. It was just their luck that the picture was lot number one hundred and eighty one. So they had to sit through two hours of boring lots passing through the sale: endless scratched sideboards and chairs with wonky legs, chipped ornaments and dirty lampshades, electrical goods that may or may not work, old bicycles, brass bedsteads and all manner of this and that. Mrs Taylor bought three CD's, a socket set for Mr Taylor and a kitchen clock. Emma bought a pot elephant, a teddy cookie jar, a large box of books and an Abba tape. Kerry didn't buy anything but clung tightly to her purse waiting, none-too-patiently, for lot one-eight-one to be displayed.

She felt the excitement mounting as the number went up to a hundred and eighty. Emma also started fidgeting, two pin points of colour rising on her cheeks. Both girls were gripped by a *rightness* with the picture...

"And now, ladies and gentlemen, we have lot one-eight-one. Look at this lovely picture. Wouldn't it look elegant above your fireplace? You never know, it might turn out to be a Rembrant. Who will give me just one pound for this delightful picture?"

Kerry's hand shot up, and she couldn't stop herself from jiggling on the seat.

The auctioneer noticed Kerry's hand and looked at Mrs Taylor for confirmation of the bid. She nodded.

"One pound to the little lady over there. Two pounds? Am I bid two pounds?"

An elderly lady in a huge fur coat waved her program to indicate a bid. Kerry scowled at her.

"Fur is worn by beautiful animals and ugly women," whispered Emma cheekily. Mrs Taylor frowned at her daughter, but Kerry, engrossed in the bidding, didn't even hear Emma's cheeky remark.

"Two pounds I have, am I bid three?"

Kerry put up her hand, so did a large man with a notebook and pen. Mrs Taylor whispered that he was probably a dealer with a market stall or second hand shop somewhere.

The auctioneer looked at Mrs Taylor again and accepted Kerry's bid as being the first. Emma jiggled in her seat with excitement.

"Three pounds I have, four pounds? Am I bid four pounds?"

The auctioneer looked at the man who had bid against Kerry. He gave a small shake of the head, indicating that he was no longer interested. Then he turned in his seat to face the girls. Kerry had been glaring at him fiercely; the man had probably felt her eyes willing him not to bid.

He raised his hat and smiled at them. Both girls smiled back and he nodded his head courteously at Mrs Taylor.

The lady in the dead rabbit had raised her hand.

"I have four pounds, am I bid five?"

Kerry bid five pounds.

The lady bid six.

Kerry bid seven.

The lady bid eight. Mrs Taylor gave her daughter a look that warned she would intervene soon and stop her bidding. It was getting too expensive.

"Am I bid eight Pounds?"

He looked at the lady. She didn't raise her pamphlet. Kerry's cheeks were burning. This was it. She was going to get the picture.

The auctioneer looked around the room, scanning every single person to make sure he hadn't missed a bid.

"Come on, folks, seven pounds for this beautiful picture. I'm giving it away. Why, this picture probably hung in Windsor castle before the great fire."

"And during!" shouted someone in the crowd. Everybody laughed. Everybody, that is, except Emma and Kerry, who were both far too interested in whether anybody else was going to place a bid.

"Okay, have it your own way, but it breaks my heart to let it go for that price, a lovely antique like this. It's probably, ooh, at least ten years old. Come on, people, make an old man happy. I have a wife and seven hungry kids to feed. Will anybody give me eight pounds for this lovely picture?"

No response.

"Going once!"

He raised his hammer.

"Going twice!"

He prepared to bring the hammer down. His arm was already into its downward swing when the lady with the fur finally made up her mind and waved her pamphlet. Kerry was furious that the bid was back with the woman.

"Ladies?"

He looked at the girls and their mum.

"Will you give me nine pounds?"

Without any hesitation, Kerry raised her hand and waved it madly. The auctioneer smiled.

"Nine pounds over here, Ladies and Gentlemen, with our pair of lovely art lovers. Who will give me ten pounds? Ten pounds, just ten measly pounds. I ask you, what does that buy these days? Come on, ten pounds for this spectacular picture. Going once!"

He raised his hammer.

"Going twice!"

He started the swing down.

Kerry began to panic. She felt sure that awful woman was going to steal the bid from her again. She got confused and then she got excited, and, almost without realising she'd done it, she flung her hand up in the air again.

"Here. Oh, here, please," she said, desperately waving her arm and jumping up out of her seat. Everybody in the place roared with laughter, but Kerry didn't care. She just had to have the picture. It was so perfect for the magic frame. Mrs Taylor went crimson and the auctioneer could hardly speak for laughing.

"My dear, the bid was already with you. You have just bid against yourself. I think you deserve this picture. I hope it brings you much happiness. To the young lady with the

*pretty smile, going with her previous bid of nine pounds!
Sold."*

He brought the hammer down with an especially
loud crack and wiped a tear of laughter from his eye.
Kerry was pink with pleasure.

"You big dope, fancy bidding against yourself. You're
lucky he didn't make you pay twice," Emma said. Kerry
was beaming and didn't care about anything but seeing
how the print would look in the frame.

*

"Ooh, just think of all those slugs climbing on your
face while you're asleep," said Mark, who was still teasing
Vicki, now that he realised he was not in immediate
danger of receiving a Chinese burn. Kerry was jolted back
to the present. She had spent some time that morning
cutting the print to size and fitting it in the frame. Now
she stood and put it in its place on the mantelpiece. They
all sat back to admire the new, completed picture.

"It's really pretty, and I can't wait to *be* there," Vicki
said. None of them gave a second thought to how silly
that would have sounded to somebody who didn't know
about the frame.

Vicki was right. It was a very pretty picture. A hill
sprinkled with buttercups and daisies filled the fore-
ground. On the top of the hill, looking like a giant over-
seer, stood a huge oak tree, its boughs spanning to give
shade from both a fierce sun and a bitter wind. Mottled
with the reflection cast from the leaves, a magnificent
horse sheltered beneath the overhanging branches. He
was a large horse, if the picture gave an accurate perspec-
tive. Behind the horse and tree, in the background of the

print, an impressive house tried to change the focal point from the horse to itself. It very nearly succeeded.

"Wow, look at the horse. Isn't he a beauty?" Mark said.

The one thing that Mark and Vicki did agree on was their love of animals. Mrs Forest always had to tell them, no, they *could* not have the cat and its nine kittens, advertised as free to a 'sucker' with a good home, nor, indeed, the unwanted dog and its five hundred fleas. Nor the hamster that would chew through a pile of laundry as fast as Mark could chew through a chocolate bar. Vicki, ever the drama queen, would threaten suicide. This made Mark grin happily and hopefully for a moment as he thought of the extra helping of pudding that just might come his way next tea-time. But, then realising that she was not serious, he would go back to sulking over the latest stray or unloved animal that would *not* be taking the Forest surname.

"Well?" said Emma, "should we do it?"

They all agreed that yes, they should.

Over the previous two weeks, while a search was in progress for a new picture, the children had made several more leaps onto Liberty Island. This was so that they could learn more about how the magic worked. They had established the time laws. One hour leap time was equal to five minutes real time. This never altered. They had also discovered that the leap force only took them all if they were standing close together, otherwise it only took the chanter. This had proven useful for sending one of them back to check things were all right at home. They had been careful to plan the time difference so that they had always leaped when the Island was closed for the night, as this would save any awkward questions being asked. Now, they were quite expert at leaping backwards and forwards and had become used to the extraordinary feeling of zapping through time and space.

"Let's do it!" said Mark.

They joined hands, as they'd discovered it was safer that way. The second time that they leaped home Kerry had been just a little too far away and was left behind. She panicked at finding herself alone on the Island and couldn't remember the trigger verse. The others had felt very sorry for her when they went to the rescue. Kerry had been terrified and hysterical at the thought of being stranded alone on the island. Since then, they had each leaped alone, so that if they ever found themselves stranded they wouldn't be scared. They had all memorised the trigger verse.

Each of them could feel the excitement pulsing through the next one's hand as they stood in front of the picture. They began the chant in unison:

Here is an image for you to keep.
Follow where the lizards leap.
Move with caution, take a peep,
Beware! Do not get in too deep.

Repeat the words inscribed below,
Take a breath and off you go.

Sand Lizard. Sand Lizard, cautiously creep.
Shim. Sham. Shally wham. Lizards leap!

When the world stopped spinning they were in for quite a surprise.

They stood and stared at each other with eyes agog and couldn't quite believe what they were seeing. The girl's leggings and tops had magically disappeared. They were now wearing frilly dresses that stopped half way between their knees and ankles. They had long white stockings on and black boots with buttons up the front.

Mark looked even more ridiculous. His jeans and Berok top had vanished. He was dressed instead in a floppy, wheat-coloured shirt and sand-coloured trousers that stopped just below his knee. Like the girls, he wore long white socks and had black shoes with buckles on the front.

Emma, for the moment forgetting that she looked daft herself, was the first to burst into hoots of laughter. "Look at Mark. He looks like Dick Wittington. Where's your talking cat, Dick? Did it run away when it saw how stupid you look?"

"Well, if I'm Dick Wittington, you are Little-Bo-Peep. Huh, you can't even look after a few old sheep without losing them."

"Look at me! Just look at me!" Vicki had a face like thunder.

"She's not happy," Emma said.

"Seriously dis-chuffed," agreed Kerry.

"Miffed as a muffin," said Mark.

Then a look passed over his face, a look they all knew, and they saw it often enough. The girls braced themselves for what they knew was coming next.

"I'm-," Mark began.

"Hungry!" the girls said in unison.

Mark was going to elaborate in detail, about just *how* hungry he was when his attention was directed elsewhere.

In all the distraction with the clothes they had completely forgotten about the horse in the picture.

However, the horse was more than interested in *them*. His head was lowered and he was pawing the ground like an angry bull. Vicki knew a lot about horses. She subscribed to *My Pony*, a magazine all about horses and ponies. She was saving up to buy a horse, but every time she had more than a pound saved something else came up and she spent it.

"It's going to charge," she said confidently.

Nobody saw any reason to doubt her, including the horse. He let out an almighty scream that didn't sound as though he was saying, "Oh how very nice to meet you, welcome to my field." Then he set off at a gallop down the hill.

"RUN!" Mark shouted, rather unnecessarily.

They had already begun to do so. They tore down the hill. At the bottom, running parallel to the tall hedge was a wide ditch full of muddy water.

Emma was slightly behind the others. She was running so fast that her body couldn't keep up with her legs.

"Steady on, legs." This was one of her favourite sayings. She risked a look behind her. The horse was not only going faster than she was, but he was also getting closer.

"Scrap that, legs, *go, go, go!*" She redoubled her effort and managed to go a little faster to catch up with the others.

"Quick, into the ditch," Mark said. The horse was now nearly on top of them.

"I am *not* going in that dirty water," whined Kerry, going towards the water nonetheless.

"Just do it, Kez, or you're going to be horse mush," Mark rasped at her.

The horse had almost caught up with them. They all jumped into the ditch and were just in time to see the horse's fawn belly sail right over their heads. They heard it land on the other side of the fence and gallop off across the next field.

"Phew!" said Emma shakily. "That was close! I didn't fancy being horse chowder. We c-c-could have been killed!"

Four heads popped up to peer out of the muddy beck. They weren't sure whether the big horse would turn around and jump back over. Tentatively, they climbed out of the ditch and stood at the bottom of the hill trying to clean themselves up a bit.

If there was one thing that Kerry hated above all else, it was being dirty. She prided herself on always looking neat and tidy and having clean nails and shiny well-groomed hair. Now, she stood dripping wet, muddy, and bedraggled.

"Well, this is not funny," she moaned, "I've probably caught fifty horrible diseases from that filthy water. I hope I don't die. I'm not going to die, am I?" Her bottom lip began to wobble and the others rolled their eyes. Kerry didn't like being dirty.

A figure came running down the hill towards them. He was a boy of about fourteen or fifteen. He was dressed in a fashion similar to Mark but was a lot scruffier than Mark had been to begin with. As he drew closer they saw that he had straw-coloured hair and deep blue eyes.

He was out of breath and his cheeks were bright red with exertion. Vicki's eyes opened as wide as saucers and she nearly swooned on the spot.

"Typical, flippin' typical," she hissed to Emma, "the best looking boy I've seen in months and I have to look like Little Miss Muffet, the mud wrestler."

Vicki smiled widely as the boy stopped beside them. She twisted a strand of wet hair round her finger and hoped he wouldn't notice the state she was in.

"Hello, I don't suppose you've seen a big chestnut stallion have you? He's escaped and if I don't find him I'll be beaten to within an inch of my life."

"Seen it?" Emma said sarcastically. "Not only have we seen it, but we nearly ended up under it. The bloomin' thing chased us all the way down the hill."

The boy blushed. "Oh, I'm sorry about that, Miss. Fly is a bit spirited. I hope none of you were hurt. I can see you are a bit of a mess."

Now it was Vicki's turn to blush. "We don't always look like this, you know. I'm normally dead trendy. I dress *Techno*."

The boy looked confused and frowned. "You're normally dead? Oh, Miss Trendy, I hope you haven't been ill. How awful for you to have almost died. Was it the consumption?"

"Eh?" said Vicki.

The others laughed. Mark laughed so hard that he almost wet himself. The boy smiled at him then whispered to Vicki, "Is he a bit feeble-minded? There's a boy in the village that's feeble-minded too."

Mark had a wicked and infectious laugh. Sometimes it completely took him over, and it was impossible not to join in when he had one of his deep, hysterical belly laughs. Soon everyone would be laughing with him even if the original source of the humour was not funny.

Tearing himself away from Mark's fit of merriment the boy seemed to suddenly remember the missing horse. "Listen, I'm sorry, but I really must go. I'm going to be in terrible trouble if I don't find Shoo-fly."

"Shall we help you?" asked Vicki, who had no intention of letting him get away *that* easily.

"I am not-" Kerry began.

"*Shut up*, Kerry!" the three cousins yelled together.

The boy said that he would be really grateful for all the help he could get. They set off together with Vicki walking as close to her new friend as possible. For the next hour they tramped over the fields trying to corner Shoo-fly. The horse would let them get right up close to him and then he would show them the whites of his eyes and put his ears back until they were flat against his head. Vicki said that this was a sign of anger in a horse, and Tom - as it turned out the boy was called - looked impressed with her knowledge. The horse would then turn his back to them, kick mud in their faces, and take off again.

They sat down on the grass to think. Vicki was furious that Tom had sat beside Kerry. She watched him as he tore off a stem of juicy grass, put it in his mouth, and began chewing on it thoughtfully. She copied him but was so busy watching Tom that she didn't notice that *her* stem of grass had a large blob of Cuckoo-spit attached to it. As Vicki came to find out only too well, it was horrible stuff - a bubbly secretion from a bug called the Froghopper. The little insect would attach itself to a blade of grass and then blow foul tasting bubbles. These cover it and keep birds from eating the bug. The cuckoo–spit was smeared all over Vicki's lips. She shot up and began spitting on the grass. This was hardly the impression that she wanted him to have. She would like to have come across as lady-like and grown up, and maybe even a little bit sophisticated. They all laughed at her, and, as usual, Mark laughed longest and hardest. Tom offered Vicki a hankie. Through her discomfort - and fear that she was going to die from Cuckoo-spit poisoning, much aided by Kerry, the Prophet of doom, - she noticed that his eyes went all crinkly when he laughed. Tom assured her that the goo was quite harmless and that she would be okay. This time, when she sat down, she managed to wriggle herself in on the other side of Tom.

They sat in silent thought for a few minutes, and then Vicki had an idea.

"Hey," she said, turning to Tom, "have you seen *The Horse Whisperer* video?"

"The what?" said Tom, looking puzzled.

"Well, never mind. It's about this man, right? And he's dead good with horses, right? Anyway, he does this thing to catch them, right? He chases one for a bit, and then when it looks at him, he turns his back and walks away from it. Then it gets curious and walks up to him and wants to be friends, right? Why don't you try it?"

"Right!" said Tom

Apart from boy bands and driving everyone nuts with her singing, which she did far too much and far too often, Vicki's other great love was animals. She was Doctor Doolittle with ponytails and fully intended to become a vet one day.

Tom looked doubtful, but he said he would give it a go. He chased Shoo-fly around for a few minutes, then he turned his back and walked away, never once looking back at the animal. When he had walked about twenty yards, he stood very still with his back to the horse. Shoo-fly whickered. It sounded as though he was saying, "Hey, I was enjoying that game. Don't you want to play anymore? Why aren't I the centre of attention?"

After a few minutes a huge shadow fell over Tom's right shoulder and he felt Shoo-fly's soft nose nudging him. Tom turned around slowly and slipped the halter that he had brought with him gently over the horse's head.

"Yeeesss!" the four cousins said in unison.

Tom looked very pleased with himself. So did Shoo-fly. They began the fairly long walk back to the, Big House, as Tom called it. He let Mark lead the horse and Mark felt very important. Tom was worried that he was going to be in terrible trouble. He told them that he had only had the job for a week, and that his mistress was a cruel and nasty lady.

"Mistress? That sounds goofy. Do you mean your teacher?" Emma asked. They were all confused.

"No, Miss Emma, I mean the lady who employs me. Wicked she is and she thinks naught of hitting me with her riding crop."

"You talk funny," said Mark rudely.

"You look funny," answered Tom, glancing down at the mud-splattered boy. They grinned good-naturedly at each other.

Kerry had been thinking. "Tom, what year is it?"

"1884, Miss Kerry, don't you know?"

"Don't be daft! It's 1999, and even *I* know that," Mark said grandly.

Now the strange clothes and Tom's odd manner of speaking all made sense. The children had leaped over a hundred years into the past! This was a little scary, but also very exciting.

That explains why Tom doesn't know what a video is, Vicki thought. The cousins fell silent for a little while as they mulled over this new information. Vicki was the first to speak. By this time she had a huge crush on Tom and wanted him to keep talking to her.

"Tom, why is the horse called Shoo-Fly? It's a pretty name."

"Ah," said Tom. "Mr Grimes, the head groom, told me the story of this last week. When they bred Shoo-fly he was just called Fly. He was a greedy colt, and when Mr Grimes took him his bran mash before bedding him down of a night, Fly would have his head in the pail before Grimes had set it down. Mr Grimes would push him off and say, "Shoo-Fly," and the name stuck."

Tom told them lots of interesting things about his life as a stable lad at Holker Manor. He started work very early in the morning, before it was even light, and never finished until after it was dark. Sometimes in summer if any of "the family" wanted to ride late, he had to work until they came in. He was given two meals a day and was paid just one shilling a week. Tom told them that he lived in the stable with the horses. He had a space in the hay-loft.

"Where do you plug in your stereo?" Vicki asked.

"What's a stair-ee-oo, Miss Trendy?" Tom said, once again confused by this strange girl.

"Oh, never mind, and my *name's* Vicki." She shook

her head. He might be good looking for an older boy, but because he came from another age he was very odd sometimes. Vicki had her doubts that he would get on well with the gang at school.

Soon they were at the rear gates of Holker Manor.

"Goodbye, then. Thank you for helping me to catch Fly. I'll remember what you showed me for next time, Miss Vicki."

They said goodbye to Tom and watched him walk the horse up the gravel path that led to the stables. Vicki sighed deeply.

"Vicki's in *lurve*," teased Mark.

"Oh, well, shall we go home for lunch?" Kerry said. Mark's eyes lit up.

*

Emma wandered into the kitchen. Nanna was loading the dishwasher, humming to herself.

"Nanna, how much was a shilling in old money?"

"Well, let me think now. It's a long time ago, you know. Twelve pence, that's right, twelve pennies made up one shilling. Why do you ask, darlin'?"

"Oh, you know, just wondered."

She shook her head as she counted all the hours that Tom had to work for his measly twelve pence. She thought of Tom and was sad to think that he had already died a long time ago.

"Vicki has got a huge crush on a ghost," teased Emma. She smiled, knowing that soon she would use that to her advantage and Vicki's embarrassment.

Suddenly she felt very tired and yawned.

"Early to bed for you tonight, young lady," said Nanna.

Chapter Four
Big Red Spots And Consequences.

Emma was in a grump.

Mark had gone fishing with his dad and granddad, and Kerry had gone to see a production of *Swan Lake* with her Mum; so they wouldn't be at Granddad's until after lunch the next day. Vicki was going out for the afternoon with her friend Rachel, that left Emma on her own with nothing to do and nobody to do nothing with.

Emma was in a grump because she was bored. The four had made a pact that none of them would ever do a leap without the others knowing. If one of them did and anything went wrong, then nobody would know where the person was, that could be very dangerous. She would be a little bit scared going on a whole adventure by herself anyway. She didn't want to read and she didn't want to play with the Playstation. In fact, she was that way out with herself and didn't know what she wanted ... or maybe she did.

Vicki and Rachel were standing in the hall getting ready to go out. They were going into town to buy the new *Leona* CD, then they were going to go bowling and have a milkshake. They felt very grown up.

"Can I come with you, please, Vic?" Emma asked.

"You won't be allowed."

"Yes, I will. Nanna said I can go if it's alright with you two."

"Well, it isn't," said Vicki spitefully.

"I'll tell Nanna you've got make-up in your bag, and you're going to put some on in town."

"Ooh, you little snitch," Vicki hissed. "I'll tell Nanna that you stole a chocolate bar when you were six."

"That was four years ago, and I've never stolen anything since." Emma's lower lip wobbled. She was ashamed of what she had done even though she had really been too young to know better. She didn't want her nanna to be disappointed in her. It was stalemate and both girls knew it.

Vicki and Rachel passed a look between them that Emma didn't notice.

"Okay then," Vicki said, "you can come, but you had better go upstairs and get changed. You're not coming with us looking like that."

Emma beamed. Sometimes her cousin wasn't so bad after all. She ran up the stairs two at a time and flew into her room where she quickly flung her wardrobe open. She pulled out her new black trousers and a pink top and changed hurriedly. It would not be wise to keep the girls waiting when they had reluctantly agreed to let her go with them.

"Vicki? Rachel?" she called out, after hurtling back down the stairs.

The rotten pair had tricked Emma and had run off down the street without waiting for her.

She thought about going after them, but by now they had probably reached the main road and Emma wasn't allowed to go there by herself. She ran to tell her nanna what had happened.

"Oh, aren't they horrible?" Nanna said. "Never mind, you can help me bake a chocolate cake for tea later. And you can lick the bowl out without having to share it with the others." Two years ago that would have been enough to make things up to Emma, but now, she was older and she wanted to be doing what the older girls did. Licking bowls out was for kids… and her Granddad, if he got there first.

Emma stomped up to her bedroom. She was furious with Vicki. Sitting on her bed, she brushed away big, fat, angry tears.

"Don't get mad, get even," she said to herself.

Emma wasn't a nasty child but she did have a temper and anybody who crossed her got to know about it one way or another. She got out her writing pad and pen and began composing a not-very-pleasant letter to her cousin:

Dear Vicki,

I think running off like that without me was horrible. It was cruel and it hurt my feelings. You're that female dog word that we're not allowed to say.

You are nasty. And I hope you get run over by a big, red, double-decker bus.

From Emma, with no love or kisses.

Emma sat back to look at her handiwork. She felt a little better. But, as she looked at the note, she did begin to feel a *bit* guilty. Maybe it was too strong. The more she looked at it, the less she liked it. So she took her pen and ran a thick blue line through the words 'big, red, double-decker bus' and, instead, wrote:

Okay, maybe not a double- decker bus, just a single one will do.

Again, she sat and looked at what she'd written. And again she got a little pang of guilt. *After all*, she thought, *would Vicki get any less squished by a single-decker bus than a double?*

She ran another line through the last sentence and wrote:

I hope you wake up tomorrow morning covered in big red spots, so that none of the

boys in school will fancy you.

There, that's much better, she thought. She read it through again, and then, as an afterthought, added:

And I hope you have a snotty nose for three weeks.

Finally satisfied with her work she placed the letter on her bookcase. As she opened her bedroom door it flew into the air and fluttered down onto the carpet beside her. She bent down and put it back on the bookcase. Again it fell down and again she picked it up. Then she stood and watched and it stayed exactly where she had put it. Well, it did until she turned around, and then once again it fluttered down onto the carpet beside her.

Suddenly, Emma had an idea. To really make the letter get Vicki's attention she would put it in the lizard frame. This would keep it secure and would make sure that it was the first thing Vicki saw when she walked into the room. It was no big deal fitting something in the frame. All you had to do was twist two grips and lift the back off.

Once she had fitted the letter, Emma felt quite pleased with herself. She wanted Vicki to know how much she had upset her. As she thought about what her cousin had done to her, she became quite angry again. She stamped her foot and said out loud, "Vicki, I am *so* mad with you, and I'm not going to forget what you did to me today."

Emma stood there fuming until she ran out of words. She opened her mouth several times but nothing came out, so she stamped her foot in temper and said the first thing that came into her head:

"Sand Lizard. Sand Lizard, cautiously creep.
Shim. Sham. Shally wham. Lizards leap!"

The room didn't spin, of course. She hadn't said the whole verse, and anyway, there was no picture in the frame. She couldn't go inside a letter, could she? But the room *did* give a little jolt. Emma shuddered, feeling nervous. She was glad she hadn't said the whole verse; maybe she would have found herself walking along next to life-sized commas or something. Even so, an odd little twinge of worry stayed with her for the rest of the day. Something didn't feel good and it wasn't stomach-ache. Emma couldn't get that odd little jolt out of her mind.

While she was out, Vicki had a fit of the guilts about Emma too and couldn't stop thinking about the mean trick she had played on her cousin.

"We were rotten to her, weren't we?" she said to Rachel. "I was so bothered about having a ten-year-old hanging around with us that I didn't stop to think about her feelings."

"Who cares," said Rachel, "she's just a kid, forget about her. She'll be playing with her dolls by now."

"Well, I wouldn't like anyone to do that to me," said Vicki.

She spent the last of her money buying Emma a pretty blue hair slide to make up for being so nasty to her.

When she got home, Vicki was in big trouble for what she had done to Emma and she was grounded for the rest of the weekend. For once, she didn't make a fuss. Vicki gave Emma the slide and said that she was sorry for being horrible. Suddenly, Emma felt very guilty too. It *was* a lovely present, and Vicki obviously meant what she said. Emma ran upstairs quickly to take the letter out of the frame before Vicki saw it. She hastily stuffed it into her trouser pocket and returned the frame, with the horse picture back inside, to Kerry and Mark's room before anybody noticed. She felt better but still had a feeling that things weren't quite right. Again, she remembered the way the room had jolted.

*

"Vicki, will you get out of that bed right this *minute*! I've called you three times and your breakfast is going cold," Nanna shouted.

Emma had nearly finished her breakfast by the time Vicki came slowly into the dining room, still in her pyjamas. She looked very sorry for herself. Her hair was sweaty and tangled, and she didn't even have the energy to hold her head up properly.

"Nanna, I don't feel well," she whined.

"Oh, good grief, sweetheart, you're covered in big red spots!"

Nanna and Granddad were so busy fussing round Vicki that they didn't notice Emma had gone very quiet and pale. Granddad went to call the doctor out while Nanna took Vicki back to bed. It looked as though Vicki had caught chickenpox.

Emma got up from the table and ran to the bathroom. She was rather forgotten in all the fuss of the doctor's visit. Doctor Watkins stood over Vicki, and, after he had taken her temperature and blood pressure, he checked her tonsils and listened to her chest. He said that it probably wasn't chickenpox. He thought it was more likely to be an allergic reaction to something she had eaten. After much discussion by the adults - while Vicki lay very still on the bed feeling poorly - they decided the culprit was probably the strawberries they'd had for dessert the night before. Doctor Watkins said that she would feel awful for the following twenty-four hours or so, but after that would be just fine. Vicki lay there with her nose streaming, looking like a dot-to-dot picture in a child's activity book.

After the doctor had gone, Vicki needed to use the bathroom. She trundled across the hall with her dressing gown, belt trailing behind her. As she closed the bathroom door, she didn't immediately see Emma sitting on the floor in the corner. When she *did* see her, she jumped high enough to nearly hit the ceiling.

Emma had her back pressed up against the wall and her arms_wrapped around her legs, with tear-wet knees hugged tightly to her chest. She rocked slowly backwards and forwards and she was making funny little moaning noises in the back of her throat. She lifted her face and tears streamed down both cheeks. When she saw Vicki, her shoulders shook and she sobbed even harder.

Vicki knelt beside Emma, putting an arm around her shoulders and pulling her close. Emma was freezing cold and shaking. She cried into Vicki's shoulder.

"Emma? What's the matter?"

"Y-y-you could have been killed by a b-b-bus. You c-could have been killed by a bus, and it's all m-m-my fault!"

"Emma? What are you talking about? Are you ill? You aren't making any sense. I'm going to call Nanna."

"No, don't do that." Emma showed Vicki the piece of paper with the letter on it. Vicki read it through and the implications gradually sunk in. She had felt sick before, now she felt sicker than ever. Neither of them spoke for some time.

"We've got to get rid of the frame, Vic," Emma finally said.

"The others will be here after lunch. Come to the bedroom and we'll all talk about it then."

*

The four children sat looking at the frame in a completely new light. Emma, who was still very shaky, was the first to speak.

"We've got to burn the frame. It's evil. Vicki could have been killed."

"No, Emma," Kerry said. "The frame isn't evil. It was your thoughts towards Vicki that were evil."

Emma hung her head and started to cry again.

"Now, look what you've done, Kerry," Vicki said. "But I do agree with you, though. The frame only did what was asked of it. We need to be very, very careful with the frame in future. I have to tell you, the thought of what might have happened gives me a cold feeling where my stomach *wouldn't* have been if that bus had got me."

"It's too dangerous. I still say we burn it, and then it can never hurt anybody," Emma said.

"No," Kerry said. "What do you say, Vicki? Mark?"

"I agree with Kerry," Vicki said.

Mark wasn't sure what he thought, but he nodded his head anyway.

The children sat quietly, each one going over their own thoughts. After a long time, Emma spoke again, now with an air of authority. She had her face set in that stubborn expression of hers that said there was no way she was going to back down, and there was no point any of them trying to make her.

"Okay, then, but if you *won't* burn it, we have no choice. We have to do something to protect ourselves from the possibilities of what might happen. I didn't for one second *really* want to hurt Vicki. I was just angry. Maybe next time we'll do something without even meaning to, and without thinking it through properly, that will set off other bad things. I suggest that we go and see Sylvia."

Emma could be stubborn and would not budge an inch if she felt she was in the right about something. She was also the one most likely to jump to the defence of the others in times of trouble. Her shyness could be momentarily forgotten when she stood up for what she knew to be - or believed to be - right. She knew she had to do *something* about the frame.

"No way," said Mark, shaking his head vigorously.

"Are you mad? The woman's a loony." Vicki instinctively rubbed her arm where that strange woman had grabbed her.

"If you won't come with me, I'll go by myself." Emma was scared but determined. She was terrified of Sylvia, but the thought of what she had nearly done to Vicki scared her a whole lot more.

"I agree," said Kerry in a small, scared voice. "I think we should go. Sylvia might be able to tell us more about the frame and how to keep ourselves safe. I'm not going to take the frame with us, though. She's not going to take it off us." Kerry stuck out her chin with a look of stubborn determination that easily equalled Emma's.

"That's settled then. As soon as Vicki's better, we go and see Sylvia."

Chapter Five
From Whence She Came

The fearless four stood at the gates of Brampton Hall. They were doing a good impression of being anything *but* fearless; in fact, anyone looking on would be excused for thinking they were terrified.

In front of them was a pair of huge wrought iron gates. They were as tall as two large adults - one on top of the other - and had wicked looking spikes on the top. Worked cleverly into the ironwork was a crude picture of a road leading through a valley, and above this some wording in the form of an arc.

"From Whence they came," read Vicki. It didn't make any sense to her. She thought it sounded a bit sinister, almost like some sort of warning to turn back. She took out her hanky and blew her runny nose.

To the left of the main gates was a much smaller one. What they call, in country villages, a kissing gate.

"Oh, let's go home. This is daft," Vicki said.

Kerry agreed with her. "I want to watch my *Walking with Dinosaurs* video."

"My mum was making beef pie for tea," Mark stated hopefully.

Emma sighed loudly. "Okay, fair enough, give up and go home then. Go on, off you go."

The others whooped with joy and relief. They turned and began walking back down the hill towards home, and comfort and safety.

"Oh-oh, hey, you two," Kerry said. "Somebody isn't with us."

The three reluctant children turned around, already knowing what they were going to see. Sure enough, Emma had gone through the gate and was already striding stubbornly up the drive. On her own!

"Oh no," Vicki said, before shouting after Emma, "Hang on, Em! Wait for us!"

"I knew you were going to say that. I just knew it." Mark looked longingly towards home, rooted to the spot. He looked towards the dark, scary mansion and then looked down the hill again. This was a nightmare of indecision. He took one last, wistful look - wondering if he would ever see his lovely home again - and then he set off at a run to catch up with the others. He comforted himself with the thought that if the crazy woman did lock him in a cage with the intention of eating him for Christmas lunch, then at least she would fatten him up first. As a precaution before they set off, he had hidden a letter inside his Mickey Mouse pyjama case. It said:

Dear Mum and Dad,
I have been capshurd and eaten by the wickid witch of Bramton Hall. Maybe the Police will find me in time cuz I mite not have been eaten just yet. If I do get out in time can I have Lsanya for tea please this will help me to get better. Don't throw my toys out. I love you.
Mark.

He caught up with the girls and they all walked slowly up the huge gravel drive. They tried to walk quietly so that Sylvia wouldn't hear them coming and let a pack of savage dogs out to get them. Unfortunately, Vicki sneezed loudly, ruining the plan, but the gravel still crunched loudly under their feet anyway. The gardens were a wilderness. Off to their right was a wooded area. The children walked all the way over to the left, as *anything* could leap out from that wood and grab them. On the left hand side of the drive was what had at one time been the stately lawns, but these days were little more than an overgrown mass of wild grasses and weeds. The flowerbeds had long since overflowed and lost all their form, and what was either a bird bath or a fountain in the centre, had grass growing right past the rim of its bowl so that it was almost invisible.

All too soon they rounded the last corner and were standing in an open circle leading up to an enormous, gothic main door. The front porch itself could have been beautiful - honeysuckle, cyclamen, and climbing roses framed the archway - but the pretty, nice smelling flowers were being suffocated and killed by dark green ivy. The children didn't see beauty; they only saw danger and menace.

Emma raised her hand to pull the rope that rang the bell. The others all shrank back; ready to run if the need arose. She had just wrapped her fingers around the rope when suddenly the door was flung wide open and Sylvia stood on the threshold in a mass of swishing skirts.

The children were all so shocked and taken by surprise that they backed up, partly through fear, and partly because they had no choice as Sylvia took up most of the room on the small porch. Mark stumbled over his feet, which seemed to have somehow become tangled with the step, and he fell sprawling on the floor. Kerry tottered into a branch of the climbing roses and ivy. It snagged her new black woolly tights. She put her finger on the snag to feel if she was bleeding and an enormous ladder ran down her leg, leaving a finger sized hole where the snag had been. She was *not* impressed; the tights had been labelled 'ladder resistant'.

Suddenly, Kerry was not scared, she was *mad*. She strode right up to Sylvia and twisted her leg in a most unnatural fashion to show off her calf and the offending ladder.

"Oh, thank you very much," she began sarcastically. "Do you know these are my new tights? They cost two pounds ninety-nine pence, and now they're ruined!"

Sylvia looked down at Kerry as though she was an irritating fly buzzing round her head. She waved her hand at her dismissively. "Well, you lot took your time to get here, didn't you? Now that you *are* finally here you'd better come in. Oh, for goodness' sake, get up off the floor, Mark. You aren't hurt."

She ushered them inside the house and slammed the door loudly. The children looked at each other. How did she know Mark's name?

"Ugh," said Mark, as a cobweb floated down from a dusty old chandelier and wrapped itself around his face.

"What's the matter with you now, boy? Scared of a little-biddy spider home? And what do you suppose the *spiders* would think if they had to look at your ugly mug?"

Mark opened his mouth to speak, thought better of

it, and shut it again before anything alive and creeping crawled into it. He shrank back from the woman, too young to notice that her bright green eyes twinkled merrily as she teased him.

"Come on then, we have a lot to talk about, can't stand here all day. What time are your parents expecting you back, and do they know where you are?"

"Oh, yes, they know alright, and they'll send the police here looking for us if we aren't back by five o'clock." Mark was not only very rude to the lady, but he was also telling a whopping great lie. Their parents thought they had gone to the, Saturday Matinee Four Hour Spectacular Children's Program, at the local cinema. In fact, they had dropped the children there themselves.

"Oh, I see. Weeeelll," Sylvia said thoughtfully, "I'll have to make sure that I don't leave any evidence, won't I?" Sylvia was having great fun teasing them.

She led the way across the tiled floor of the main hall. Mark nudged Vicki in the side and pointed to Sylvia's slippers. They grinned at each other and shared the joke by pointing them out to the other two.

"I don't know what her problem is," whispered Emma, quietly, "but I bet it's hard to pronounce."

Sylvia swung around very daintily for such a big lady. "What are you sniggering at? Haven't you seen a pair of slippers before?"

For once, Sylvia's clothes almost corresponded with each other. She was wearing a long black skirt and matching top, and although she still wore the little hat on the top of her head, her usual gaudy scarf was missing. The only things that really looked out of place were her bright orange Ali Baba slippers. They were enormous and curled round like wound-up caterpillars at the tips.

The hall tapered at the far end into a long, narrow passageway, which then became a flight of steps leading downwards. These in turn led into the biggest kitchen that the children had ever seen. It was dark because there was a board nailed to the windows, presumably to keep vandals and thieves out. Sylvia turned the light on. Every surface in the kitchen was thick with dust and cobwebs and had obviously not been used in a very long time. Vicki sneezed twice, making them all jump. They could feel the dust building up at the back of their throats.

The strange woman – who, oddly, didn't really look very old anymore and had apparently lost her limp - walked lightly across the kitchen to a beam that was strung with pots and pans of all manner and description. She pulled on the third saucepan from the left and the hook moved down in a lever action. The children jumped, startled by a sudden low rumbling sound behind them. An entire wall was shifting. It opened up to reveal a passageway leading back into the house.

"Fantastic, a secret passage!" Mark exclaimed, obviously impressed.

"There are several of them all over the house, all leading to my room," Sylvia said.

They walked through the hole in the wall and down a long, dust-free, reasonably lit corridor, until they came to a door at the end. If it occurred to the children that anybody looking for them would never find anything, they didn't let on. They had passed several intersections in the passageway, but kept on moving straight ahead towards the door at the very end of the corridor. Sylvia unfastened three locks on the door with a variety of modern keys, all fished from the pocket of her skirt. The children felt very apprehensive. How would anyone ever find them down here?

"Oh, now, don't start panicking again." She seemed to read their thoughts. "You'll be back at the cinema in good time to meet your folks."

"How on earth did she know about *that*?" Mark had the good grace to blush furiously as Sylvia turned to him and winked.

They walked into a huge circular room, deep within the heart of the house.

It was amazing!

There were no windows but the room was fresh and well ventilated. It was clean, immaculately tidy, and really very nice. Around the room were six doors set into the walls. Sylvia explained that these were her escape routes; though, why she would need to escape - and from whom or what - she rather worryingly didn't say. The centre of the room was taken up with two big, curved, bright purple sofas with lots of soft fluffy cushions. They were very comfortable. At the back of the sofas, three large alcoves were set into the wall. In one was a very modern fitted kitchen, another housed a bedroom and the last contained the bathroom. Each of these rooms, within a room, had a louvered door that was pushed open. There was also a television, a music centre, lots of books arranged around the room on elegant bookcases and ornaments and knick-knacks galore. The focal point of this amazing circular room was a massive grandfather clock. Its face told the children that it was one-twenty p.m.

Sylvia took off her hat and hung it on one of the

hooks of an ornate mahogany coat stand. The children gaped in surprise and amazement. No wonder Sylvia always wore her floppy hat. She had a broad stripe of bright purple hair across the top of her head! It made her look like a punk badger.

"I know, I know. Weird, isn't it? I get it from my father's side. Typical, my mother has a lovely figure and my Dad has wacky hair and which do I get?" She pointed at her funny hair with a comical expression on her face, making the children laugh.

Sylvia went into the kitchen area. Laid out on a tray were five glasses and a pitcher of lemonade. On another plate was a mouth-watering array of cakes and biscuits. She dropped a dozen ice-cubes into the jug. Then, from the kitchen drawer she took a huge knife with a massive steel blade. She turned to the children, holding up the cleaver and moving slowly towards them. They all shrank back into the plush velvet of the soft cushions, terrified as this sinister woman with unusual green eyes advanced towards them. The knife was raised above her head. Its blade glinted in the harsh fluorescent lighting that spilled through from the kitchen. The children were terrified. They were trapped in a house, where they could never be traced, with a crazy woman who was about to kill them.

Sylvia held up the lemon, which had been concealed in her other hand.

"Lemon?" she asked, smiling.

The children gulped and nodded. Mark managed to croak out a weak, "Yes, please."

Sylvia deftly chopped thick slices of bitter lemon and dropped them into the jug of lemonade. She brought the tray over and, when they'd recovered from their shock, they all tucked into a wonderful snack of cakes and home-made lemonade. It was very good. Kerry wondered if it might be poisoned. She wasn't going to have anything, but when she saw the others tucking in without keeling over and clutching at their throats in the throes of death, it was all just too good to resist.

Only after they had all finished eating and their glasses had been re-filled with more lemonade, did Sylvia turn on Emma. Her eyes blazed with an almost unnatural green light. This time there was no mistaking the anger within the stare.

"So, young lady, you gave yourself a nasty fright, didn't you? Where would young Vicki be now if you hadn't changed that note?"

Emma hung her head in shame and her eyes brimmed with tears that she was desperately trying to keep contained. She failed, and a tear made its way slowly down her cheek. It dripped off the end of her face and plopped in to her glass of lemonade.

Sylvia was instantly sorry for hounding the little girl, but it had needed to be said. Her expression softened and the anger went out of her eyes.

"There-there, lass, it's alright now, no harm was done. But now maybe you see why I was so desperate to get the frame back. In the wrong hands that frame could cause trouble the like of which the world has never before seen. It's not a toy. You children were cursed the day you saw that piece of wood. The responsibility on you all is enormous. I could just so easily take it back, and believe me; it would be better for you if I did. But you can take that worried look of your faces. For now, at least, it's going to be safer with you. I've thought and thought, wracked my brains to come up with another solution, but I'm afraid I have to protect the frame. That is my purpose, you see. I am one of the keepers of the frame. It is my duty to protect it and keep it from harm and from falling into dangerous hands. I wish there was another way."

"What do you mean?" Emma asked. "You're *one* of the keepers of the frame? You mean there are others? Who are they? Will they try to come for it?"

"Absolutely, he will, and when he does we will be ready for him. But I'll get to all that later. I have so much to tell you and so little time. How much do you need to know? How much is it safe to tell you? How much is better left unsaid?"

Sylvia shook her head. It seemed as if she were asking herself the questions. She sat on the corner of the sofa mumbling to herself, trying to decide just what to tell them. The children were tingling with anticipation and nervousness.

"However," she continued, with an air of command completely out of the blue. "The frame can stay with you, but there *have* to be rules made and guidelines set. We have had one near catastrophe, and that's nothing to what *could* be done with the frame. Firstly, and this is the single most important rule, the frame must *never* be used to change the course of history. Now, this is going to be a difficult one for you to come to terms with and understand. With one spell you could end war, famine, disease, but it would be disastrous."

"How could that be bad?" Vicki asked, confused. She wiped her nose on a rather soggy hanky.

"Because, child, the world is set on a course that should never be altered. Destiny decides what is to be, not four children in a little English backwater. The world is a bad place right now, and that's why I'm here. I have been sent out to learn the ways of this world so that my people will never make the same mistakes."

Vicki opened her mouth to ask another question, but Sylvia held up a hand to silence her. She sneezed instead and glared at Emma for inflicting this terrible runny nose on her. Mark jiggled on his seat with unasked questions. It was no good - he couldn't contain himself. He *had* to know.

"Are you an alien, then?"

Sylvia looked at him solemnly. "Soon, child, be patient and I'll answer anything you want to know, but, for now, listen and try to understand. This is far more important than who I am. I will answer your questions later. First, you must sit quietly and listen."

She waited for each of them to calm down and settle. It was important that they paid attention to what she was telling them. They had a busy afternoon ahead, with a lot of information to take in, and she wanted to make sure that they understood each point before moving on to the next.

"*Rule 1. You must never use the frame to alter the course of history.* Man is making a terrible mess of this planet and he has to be allowed to continue to do just that. One day he will look around him at the mess he has made and will want to put it right. If something magically makes the world a wonderful place for him, then he will just make exactly the same mistakes again, and all the hundreds of years of learning that *you* have already gone through - as a race of people - will have to be repeated. Now, that doesn't mean that you can't use the frame to help individual people. It's going to take time to learn how to use the frame wisely. You can pick at little problems to make someone's day better, but you must not try to change the world.

"*Rule 2,*" she continued. "*You must never use the frame to cause harm to another living creature.* This one is self-explanatory, and I don't think any of you will be trying that one again. I know," she held up her hand at Emma's coming protest. "I know, child, you had no idea what you were doing and never wished any harm to come to Vicki really.

"*Rule 3. You must not use the frame to further your own selfish desires.* What that means is that you may use the frame and enjoy it. That is what it was made for. But you may not, for instance, use it to win the lottery. While on a leap you may take advantage of whatever comes your way, but you may not ask the frame for ridiculous material goods. Is that understood? Are all my rules understood?"

Emma, Kerry, Vicki, and Mark all agreed that they understood what had been said to them.

"Now then, before we leave this subject, I must tell you that I am going to have to do something to ensure that you stick to the rules. When you arrive home you will see that the frame has changed. Count the berries. Overnight one will be taken. This is the first penalty against the frame being used badly. Every time you misuse the frame, one berry will be taken, until none remain. When the last berry has gone, the frame will become useless to you, just another old frame. At this time it must be returned to me. This may seem like a punishment, and to some degree it is, but it is also a guide for you to learn by. You may not be sure of your actions, but if a berry is taken you will know you have done wrong. Do you understand?"

"Not really. What are the berries? And who will take them?" asked Vicki.

"You will see, child. That is not important. What *is* important is that you understand that if you waste the berries, the frame will become useless to you and must be returned."

The children all nodded.

"Right, now you may ask your questions. Fire away." Sylvia settled back in the cushions and waggled her left orange slipper, making a bell on the end of the curl tinkle.

"Are you an alien?" Mark asked, quickly. Oh, he did hope the answer was yes. He'd never met a real live alien before. Maybe she would take her skin off to show him how hideous she really was.

"No, Mark. I'm not an alien."

Mark's face fell. He made no attempt to hide his disappointment.

Before he could press the point and try to persuade her that she actually *was* an alien but just didn't realise it yet, Vicki jumped in. "Who are you?"

"Well, my real name is Silkier Taffetine Ozenga. But I'm sure you can see the advantages of using the name Sylvia Sanders while I'm staying here. You see, I don't like to draw attention to myself."

The children looked at her purple hair and bright orange slippers and tried not to look amused by her last remark. And Mark, well, he almost made it, almost, but not quite. He had just taken a large mouthful of lemonade. He had to decide between swallowing and laughing, and the laugh won. Then everybody laughed except Kerry, who sat opposite Mark with lemonade dripping off her face and into her lap.

"Where are you from?" Emma asked when Kerry had wiped her face and calmed down.

"I'm from Whence."

"Where's Whence?"

"From Whence they came," said Vicki, remembering the inscription on the gate.

"That's right, child!" Sylvia said, delighted, "From Whence I came."

"But where is Whence?" persisted Kerry.

"Through the Way."

For a few seconds none of the children could think of anything to say. They sat and looked confused. Somehow they felt as though this conversation *should* make sense, but if it did then they were missing a vital point somewhere.

"It does sound like English, but I can't understand a word you're saying," Emma remarked sarcastically.

"What's the Way?" Kerry asked.

"The Way to Whence," Sylvia replied, enjoying herself.

"Oh-oh," moaned Emma, "I'm out of my mind, but do feel free to leave a message."

"Okay, okay," Vicki butted in before Emma could make anymore of her witty remarks, "I think I've got it. The Way is the way you get to Whence, and Whence is where you came from. But where is the Way?"

"Why, it's over here, dear."

"Right," Vicki said, figuring that this was another of those rather cryptic riddles that were sending them all round in circles. "So what's 'Here'?"

Sylvia looked at Vicki as though she were stupid. "What on earth do you mean, what's here? You're here. I'm here, the house is here."

Vicki was becoming frustrated. "Oh, now you're just being silly. I'm sorry, I know you're an adult and that I have to respect you, but you are not making a lot of sense."

Kerry had been looking thoughtful during this exchange. "The Way to Whence is over here. Can you show us the Way to Whence, please?" she asked.

"Of course, dear, you only had to ask."

Sylvia got up and walked over to the old grandfather clock. "This is Granddaddy, children, and he is the Way."

The children looked at each other. Mark put his finger up to his temple and turned it. "Mad," he mouthed.

"Alright, kids, enough of this silliness." She turned around suddenly and Mark had to pretend to scratch his forehead. "Let's get back to business."

Sylvia told them to come over to her and watch carefully. She stroked her hand lovingly over the face of the grandfather clock and said:

"Grandaddy, Grandaddy, wise old Way,
Show me Whence, would you, please, today."

The face of the clock became cloudy. They couldn't see the dial any more. It was as though it was covered with a thick layer of white smoke. Sylvia ran her hand over the face again and it cleared.

What they saw made them stare in astonishment. The clock face had become like a television screen. In the screen odd-looking people were bustling about what looked like a town square. In the centre of the square sat an elderly couple. They were sitting in a sort of gazebo that was adorned with all kinds of colourful flowers. There was a queue of people waiting to talk to them. The elderly couple looked funny. They were sitting on top of a tower of books each, and their little legs dangled over the side.

The lady was very thin, with long black hair and pointed features. She wore a black dress, and red-and-green striped socks. The man was far more spectacular. He was plump, with very long hair and a beard down to his knees. Whereas Sylvia had one broad, purple stripe running from the front to the back of her head, this man had a whole host of stripes. He looked very colourful with his white and purple striped beard and hair. He wore a blue suit that finished at his knees, and orange and pink socks. They both wore boots that looked a bit like army boots, but made of felt. Perhaps the thing that made them look particularly funny was that they each had a pair of pince-nez half-glasses balanced on the ends of their noses, and they peered over the tops of them as they looked down on the people.

"*They* are my parents," said Sylvia, proudly, "Ozzie and Olivia Ozenga. They are the Olds of Whence. They were Booked to be the Whence Olds thirty years ago. Oh, it *was* a grand day. People came from miles around to see the Booking ceremony. My mother and father were chosen because they had read more Whence books than anyone else in the kingdom. This made them very wise and gave them the tallest towers. It is written in the third book of Father's tower that whomsoever has the tallest tower will be Booked to be the Whence Oldie and Oldess. Once a week the people gather in the town circle to hear their wisdom and do their bidding.

"Whence is a marvellous place. It's full of all the books that it's possible to write, all the books that will one day be written and all the ideas that someone will one day fill books with. Every time a book here in your world is written, one disappears from Whence, but it's always replaced by two more, Whence will never run out of books. The people of Whence will always be able to build their book towers, but in thirty years no one has built a higher tower than my parents. Oh, look! Look! This is going to be *good*. I want to watch this bit."

A couple moved away from the head of the queue, smiling happily. Behind them, a very odd little man shuffled forward. He was dressed in black felt army boots; tight black pants that made his skinny legs look very knobbly and a loose sort of smock-coat. He had a peculiar little face. It was shrivelled up, with a very pointy nose and chin and the beadiest little black eyes ever. His black hair was long and straggly and he looked a bit like a skinny black weasel.

"That's my brother, Adobe," Sylvia said. "He's going to get into terrible trouble. It was him who gave the frame to the school fair."

The little man threw himself down in front of the two book towers. "Oh, 'onourable olden ones," he grovelled. The children all burst out laughing at this.

"*Ssshhhh*," said Sylvia. "Listen."

"Oh, most 'ospitable, 'onourable olden ones. It was

all an 'orrible mishunderstanding. I never *meant* to give the frame to that 'orrible school fair. It just 'appened. Please say you hunderstand and will be lenient with your most hunworthy son."

"SILENCE!" boomed the man with the purple striped beard. His voice was like a deep wind instrument flooding the land with its tone. All the people in the queue shielded their faces with their arms. One lady's hat blew off, and she had to lose her place in the queue to run after it.

"How dare you insult my wisdom, you…you… you…," it seemed he couldn't think of a suitable word to describe the grovelling man, so he turned to his wife to ask about his earlier statement. "I *am* wise, aren't I, Olivia?"

"Of course you are, dear," his wife said, placating him. The little man's bottom lip had stuck out at an alarming angle and he looked as though he might cry.

"I've taken enough of your lies and deceit, Adobe Ozenga," he said, pulling himself back to the point. "I'm ashamed to call you my son. I have made excuses for you all your miserable life, but no more. It says in the forty-second book in my tower that people who do wrong should be punished. You shall be taken immediately to the Outer Wither of Whence, and there you will stay until I decide what is to become of you." A roar went up from the crowd and everybody cheered and danced.

Two large men came forward to lead Adobe away, but first they searched him and gave back all the moneybags that he had pick pocketed from the people in the queue. This was a regular occurrence on Wisdom Day. Adobe would steal everybody's moneybags and then the Whence

Policemen wouldn't know what belonged to whom. Olivia had pondered the problem for some time and then came up with something she had remembered reading in the twenty-sixth book in her pile. "If you stitch your name on all of your property, it can be returned to you if it gets lost or stolen." Everybody had oooh'd and aaah'd at her wisdom.

"Oh, *good*," said Sylvia, jumping up and down with excitement until her slippers jingled. "That gets him out of our hair for a while, but you must always be on your guard. Daddy will soon go soft and let him back from the Outer Wither, and then you must be ready because he will come after the frame. And now, I think is a good time to check on the frame, don't you?"

Sylvia ran her hand over the clock face and it clouded. She chanted:

"Grandaddy, Grandaddy, wise old Way,
Show me the frame, would you, please, today."

She wiped her hand over the glass a second time, and when the fog cleared it showed the frame with the horse picture, sitting on the mantelpiece in Kerry and Mark's bedroom at their granddad's house.

"So *dat's* how you knew so much aboud us," Vicki said, stuffily. She sneezed and blew her nose. "Doh, I *do* wish by dose would stop rudding."

Sylvia chuckled. "Granddaddy will show me anything I ask it to, so I can always check on the safety of the frame, and of you lot too. But that's not all. It can also *take* me places. Watch this. Vicki, when I've gone, see if you can remember the 'Show-me' trigger spell."

Sylvia ran her hands over the cabinet of the clock, which housed the pendulum mechanism. She chanted:

"*Grandaddy, Grandaddy, wise old Way,*
Take me to Whence, please, without delay."

The door of the clock cabinet opened, and a tunnel of bright light shone from inside. Sylvia walked into the light and disappeared. The door in the clock shut behind her and the cousins were left alone in the strange house. Vicki's hand shook slightly as she wiped it over the face of the clock. She chanted:

"*Granddaddy, Granddaddy, wise old Way,*
Show me Whence, would you, please, today."

When the face cleared, Sylvia waved at them from the end of the queue in Whence. She jumped up and down and looked very pleased with herself.

One second later she was back, looking slightly rumpled but otherwise none the worse for wear.

"Wow!" said Mark, predictably. "Oh, rats, I don't ever want to go back to being just an ordinary school-kid again, this is way too much fun."

"Now, before you go, I have one last thing to tell you. I am not allowed to just 'Way' into one of your leaps. *You* have to summon me if you need my help." She went to the side of the room and took the lid off a china ginger jar that was sitting on top of the television. Taking something out of it, she said, "Vicki, as you're the eldest-"

"How do you know," Vicki interrupted. "Oh, yes. The Way."

"As I was saying, Vicki, you take this and wear it all the time. If you need me, touch the trinket. The trigger chant is: *Sylvia, Sylvia, most beautiful woman,*
We're in a mess, we need you, so come on."

The children looked at her in disgust.

"Oh alright then," she said. "Try:
Sylvia, Sylvia, calling you,
We're in the picture, come on through." "That's
better," Mark said.

"Now, you remember, don't be calling on me every five-and-twenty minutes. I've been around this world and several others ten times and have no wish to be bailing you out every day."

She handed Vicki a gold chain with a tiny little lizard hanging from it. Vicki was going to have trouble explaining such an item to her mum, but she would deal with that when the time came. It was very beautiful.

"I got the frame. I should get the necklace," whined Kerry.

"I've got the prettiest neck, so I should get the necklace," smirked Emma.

"I don't want the blooming necklace," said Mark, and they all laughed.

Sylvia led them back through the maze of secret tunnels and out of a different door to that which they came in by. This one led out into the garden by the side gate.

"Now, think on, you lot. After you've lied to your mum about getting that cheap necklace from the hook-and-grab machine at the cinema, don't you be telling your poor mother any more of your lies. You hear? Old Sylvia will be watching you." They laughed at Sylvia's sly way of telling them what to say.

They all said goodbye and waved to her as they went out of the gate. Suddenly, Mark turned and ran back, flinging his arms around her waist, giving her a big bear-hug. "I like you, Sylvia. You're really cool for an adult."

"Get off me, you big soft fool," she said sternly. But as Mark ran to catch up with the others she had a grin from ear to ear. "Bye, Mark love," she called after him softly.

When they got back to Granddad's house, they rushed upstairs to check on the frame. Sure enough, it was different. The lizards had moved, for one thing, and on each long side of the frame, hanging from the ivy in a cluster, was a bunch of smooth shiny berries, carved from the wood. Each bunch had twelve berries in it.

"Twenty-four mistakes, gang," Emma said. "That's all. Just twenty-four visits from the mess-up fairy."

That night, before they went to bed, they were all in Kerry and Mark's room.

"Night-night, Sylvia," Emma whispered. "Say goodnight to the Wrinklies for me."

"*Olds!*" shouted the other three together.

Chapter Six
The King And Them.

There was no doubt about it. Not only had the lizard moved, but it was also grinning. The children couldn't believe their eyes. While they slept, one of the carved lizards on the frame had moved four inches down the side and had eaten one of the berries.

"So, *that's* how it was taken," Emma said. They had been wondering since leaving Sylvia's house the day before how one of the berries would be 'taken'; now, all had been revealed.

The little wooden lizard looked extremely pleased with himself. Emma touched it, running her hand all over the tiny reptile. When she ran the tip of her finger across its mouth, a single red blob dripped onto her nail. She drew back her hand, amazed. At first she thought she had pricked herself on a rough bit of wood and she stuck the finger in her mouth to suck the wound.

"Blackberry juice! I don't believe it, that was a drop of blackberry juice!"

"That's amazing," Vicki said. "Isn't it great having a magic frame? Don't forget, though, we have lost one blackberry. That means that there are only twenty-three left. We will have to be really careful not to lose any more, right?"

The children weren't happy. That evening their parents were going to see an amateur production of *The King and I* at The Coronation Hall. The four begged to go, too, but it was not going to finish until late and their parents decided that they were not allowed to go. It was exactly three weeks to the day since Emma had put the letter in the frame. That morning, Vicki had woken up with not a sniffle nor a sneeze in sight. Her red nose had cleared up 'as if by magic', and she was very relieved. It would have been nice if they could have gone to the show, especially as now she wouldn't have sneezed her way through the performance.

"I know," Mark said, "why don't we use the frame to go to the show? We have the advertising leaflet that was put through the door. If we use that it will leap us into the audience!"

They were all very excited. This was a great idea.

They had bathed and were ready for bed by seven o'clock, as it was school the next morning and they were to go straight from Nanna's house. Normally on a Sunday evening, bedtime was at nine o'clock so they had two hours to kill before their nanna started badgering them into their respective bedrooms for the night. Mark went downstairs first and said goodnight to his grandparents. He told them that he had a headache and was going to go to bed early, which wasn't a lie; he *did* have a *slight* headache and *would* have an early night. Then the girls also went down and said goodnight. They told them that they were all going to lie in bed and read their new Terry Pratchett books.

This was going to be risky. What if Nanna came up to check on them? Still, if they were gone three hours in leap time, it would only be fifteen minutes real time. It was unlikely that they would be checked on for at least an hour. And, anyway, *Coronation Street* was due to start soon, and they wouldn't be disturbed while that was on. The performance would be finished by about half past nine. When they leapt back, they would be home not much more than ten minutes after they left, even if they had had three hours in their leap. This meant that they would be home well before the end of the television program at half past seven.

The leaflet was in the frame and ready, so they all joined hands.

"Stop," said Kerry. "We can't."

"Why not?" Vicki asked, breaking the circle.

"It's against the rules. We'll lose a berry."

"No, we won't. Sylvia said we *could* use the frame to enjoy ourselves," reasoned Vicki.

"Yes, but Vicki, it's wrong. We're going to get into the show without paying. That's like stealing, and I don't think the frame would like that."

They all pondered this point. Sadly, it was agreed that Kerry was probably right. They sat on the floor in front of the frame with long faces, heads in their hands. The show was due to start in ten minutes, by now their parents would have gone in and been seated.

"I know," Kerry began, "there's a way of doing it that wouldn't be dishonest. We will leap through the frame, and then sneak back out and join the queue to pay ourselves in. If anybody says anything about us being by ourselves, we can just pretend to be with the people in front of us. Nobody will think anything of it."

It was agreed that this was a fantastic idea. They

hoped that they wouldn't lose a berry for it. They didn't think that they would but would have to check the frame when they got back, just in case. The children joined hands again and prepared to leap. They chanted the trigger together. Since Emma's accident, they had discovered that they only needed to chant the last two lines of the poem:

Sand Lizard. Sand Lizard, cautiously creep.
Shim. Sham. Shally wham. Lizards leap!

*

"Can't you children read? And don't you tell me you never saw the sign. It says, *quite* clearly, 'Do not stand in the wings unless you are waiting to go on stage'. Now, get to your dressing rooms. Look! We open in ten minutes and you aren't even ready yet!"

The angry man had appeared from nowhere two seconds after they had leaped. Where were they? The children couldn't get their bearings. This wasn't the hall. What was going on? The man was herding them down a corridor.

"James. *James*! These belong to you, I believe. I know I'm only a lowly stage manager and *you* are the musical director, but do please try and keep the blooming kids under control. I caught these four backstage, and they aren't even ready to go on yet. NINE MINUTES TO CURTAIN FOLKS!" he bellowed, and then disappeared in a flurry of flapping beige suit.

People in wonderfully bright costumes and heavy make-up were pushing past them on all sides.

"Oh no, I've lost my wig. Has anyone seen my wig?"

"*Doh, re, mi, far, soh, la, ti, doh.*"

"Now remember that third turn is to the left, not the right."

"*La, la, la, la, la, la, la,* laaaaaaaaaaaa!"

"Daaaahrling, do me up, there's a luv."

It was bedlam, so many people pushing along the narrow corridor. The man, who had taken charge of them, looked the children up and down.

"I suppose you are the four stand-ins from the agency? This flu bug is playing havoc with my children. Now, look, I know you haven't rehearsed, but you're familiar with the way it works. Yes? Luckily, they are all non-speaking parts, except one of you has just one line and the prompter will help you if you get stuck. Just follow the others and try to melt into the crowd. *SCORE! Will someone get me a score for these kids please?*" As he shouted he was already pushing them through a door on the left.

"Oh, thank goodness," sighed a lady clutching a load of theatre make-up in her hand. "The agency is cutting it fine this time. Still, you're here now." They were each guided firmly into a seat by four enthusiastic women who set about giving them an instant 'Asian' look.

The children sat in swivel chairs in front of a huge mirror. Vicki was beginning to enjoy herself immensely. Suddenly, from the other side of the room, she heard Mark's voice pipe up: "Sand Lizard, Sand Lizard…"

"*Don't you DARE!*" Vicki shouted.

Mark shut up instantly. He knew that tone of voice all to well. He tried to hang his head, knowing that all this could only end in trouble. Unfortunately, as soon as he put his head down, the woman thrust a yellowed finger roughly under his chin and forced him to tilt his face back up again. Mark had no choice but to look into the woman's hard, grey eyes. She had a smell of stale cigarettes.

When Vicki had shouted across at Mark, the make-up lady hovering over her face thought that she was talking to *her*.

"Oooh," she began, "I was only putting a bit of this of blue eye shadow on you. I suppose you *could* have the green if you prefer, but with your colouring dear, I would strongly advise the blue. You kids, one whiff of greasepaint and you all think you're flippin' superstars. I say, Jenny?" she shouted across the room to her friend. "I think we ought to curtsey to this one on the way out. All this princess stuff's gone right to 'er 'ead!"

Vicki blushed and, when she was able to open her eyes again, glared at Mark.

As soon as all four were made-up, a young man herded them back out into the corridor. "You're alright for a bit yet," he told them reassuringly. "The King's children don't go on until almost the end of the first act."

The cousins stood in the corridor with about twenty other kids who looked just like they did. They were heavily made-up to look Siamese, with jet-black wigs made from thick wool that was uncomfortably hot already. Their eyes were outlined in thick black make-up that gave them the oriental effect. They wore short satin trousers that ended at their calves, with matching mandarin jackets and black pumps. They all looked very good.

Vicki felt extremely excited. She was going on stage in *The King and I*. What a fantastic adventure!

The others were just plain terrified.

"Break a leg," shouted the woman who had attended to Mark.

"Huh? Never mind my legs missus, bet they last longer than your lungs," he muttered under his breath.

"Wonder who trod on her face?" Emma whispered.

"Never mind that," hissed Mark. "What are we going to do? We've got to get out of here! Let's see if we can find somewhere to leap without anybody noticing."

"Not likely! I've always wanted to be in a show. This is *fantastic*," Vicki said.

"Are you mad? Earth to Vicki! Come in Vicki!" said Emma, "Our parents are in the audience. You know, those mums who gave birth to us, those dads who we threw up on when we were babies? Those parents who think we are safely tucked up in our cozy little beds? I'm leaping. No 'ifs', no 'buts'. *I'm* leaping, you can do what you like."

"Well, I'm not going anywhere. I'm staying to do the show. This is a dream come true, and anyway, the folks will *never* recognise us looking like this. Just try not to gawp straight out at the audience." Vicki wasn't going to be talked out of being a star for the night, not a chance.

"I'm in," said Kerry. "It'll be fun, and like Vicki said, if we stay in the background they'll never know it's us. Why would they? They aren't expecting us to be there. What about you, Mark?"

"Dunno," he said, shuffling from one foot to the other. "I feel like a right idiot dressed like this. What if any of my mates see me? Fink I'll go home wiv Emma."

"Okay, suit yourselves, it's your loss. But I wish you'd stay, it won't be so much fun without you two. Anyway, look, everyone's gone past now. So, if you really want to, you can leap without anyone noticing. See you later," Vicki said, casually.

While the four soon-to-be-superstars were trying to work a way out of the mess they had got themselves into, four disappointed children were being turned away from the stage door by the man in the ridiculous beige suit.

"I don't care who sent you! They must have got their numbers wrong. The agency has already sent four kids out, so we won't be needing you tonight, thank you. Yes, yes, all right. You do that." He forced the children out of the door. "Don't call us, we'll call you!" he shouted cruelly as he shut the door firmly in their faces.

Mark and Emma held hands and began to chant: "Sand liz…"

"*There* you are!" the stage manager interrupted. "It's not good enough. I shouldn't have to chase around after you. If you can't be professional little act-*ors*, then you should not have your names down on the drama class temp list. You are on in thirty seconds…now *MOVE*!"

Once again, they felt themselves being pushed and prodded along the corridor until they were back in the stage wings. The other children were all filing onto either side of the stage with their arms folded. With one almighty shove, the stage manager pushed Emma and Kerry. They were standing directly behind Mark and Vicki, and the four of them flew out of the wings and onto the stage.

They were definitely in the spotlight now.

"Oh, crikey, I think I'm going to throw up," whispered Emma.

"Don't," shrieked Kerry, "please don't be sick. You

won't be sick on me, will you?" The cast on stage turned around and shushed her like a gaggle of angry geese.

Vicki instantly got the hang of it. She folded her forearms one over the other and strutted out like a true performer. The others just copied her. She seemed to know what she was doing.

The stage set was breathtaking. It was made to look like an oriental palace, with paper screens and real lanterns and cleverly painted scenery. The only prop on the stage was an easel with a map of the world. The leading lady was standing centre stage. Her character's name was Miss Anna, and in the story she had come with her son from England to teach the King of Siam's children. The King of Siam had lots of children and twenty-four of them were on the stage, as well as six of his favourite wives. Miss Anna was wearing a long blue dress with a huge hooped underskirt.

Mark was amazed that the King of Siam had so many wives. "Greedy devil, having all those wives," he whispered. Unfortunately, the front-of-stage microphones picked up his comment and took it right to the back of the hall. The audience roared with laughter.

The children just copied everybody else while they were announced by the King's eldest son and introduced to Miss Anna. Everything went without a hitch, until it was Emma's turn to go forward. A few "Ahhh's" came up from the audience when Emma was presented. Her natural shyness was assumed to be part of the performance. Emma was mortified and shuffled forward with her head bowed. She was required to kneel before Miss Anna and put her forehead on the floor in a position of Asian humility and respect. The problem was, once she got down there, the thought of having to move again in front of all those people was just too much. She had frozen to the spot. One of the King's wives had to shuffle out of line and move her.

"Psst! Kid! Move," she whispered, coming out of character, and sounding surprisingly like Mrs Clark from the chip shop.

Emma shuffled back in a half crouch, pulled unsympathetically by the King's wife. This time the audience tittered. Emma just wanted to die. It was a terrible ordeal for the shy girl. She shuffled right around the edge of the stage to hide at the back of all the children. The audience also presumed this to be a rehearsed part of the act, and the collective "Ahhhh" was even louder.

Soon the orchestra began to play the song, "Getting to Know You". All the children joined in, and their sweet, combined voices rang out clearly over the hall, bringing an appreciative tear to many an eye in the audience. They had been trained in choral singing for months and knew just the right tone to pitch their singing. There was no other word to describe it but, angelic.

Vicki had drifted off into a semi-daydream. Suddenly as the children sang the first line of the chorus, her head snapped up, her eyes widened. She tilted her head to one side like an alert budgie and listened to a few bars of the song. Then, completely forgetting where she was, she got excited. In a voice that rose above all the singing and was taken out to the audience, Vicki gasped, "Hey, I know this song!"

She could contain herself no longer. It seemed she had completely forgotten her earlier warnings about melting into the cast and not doing anything to get themselves unduly noticed. She opened her mouth wide - much wider, in fact, than anybody else on the stage - and began to sing.

Vicki gave it her all:

"Getting to know you, getting to know all about you.
Getting to like you, getting to hope you like me…"

As she became more involved with the music, her arms took on a life of their own. They extended until they were straight out in front of the children at either side of her. Vicki sang. She sang, sang, sang. Vicki sang for all she was worth. It's not as though the sound that came out of Vicki wasn't in tune, but there was nothing sweet about it. Our girl had been listening to Miss Anna's controlled, operatic voice. She could do that! She sang high. She warbled her words so that her lips wobbled like jelly and her neck looked like a turkey's. But, most of all, Vicki sang LOUD…

Five rows back, sitting in the audience, Mrs Forest wiped her eye with a hanky. She had been laughing so hard that tears were rolling down her cheeks. She dug Mr Forest in the ribs.

"Hey Grant," she asked her husband, "who does that remind you of?"

"Our Vicki," they both said in unison.

The next scene involved Miss Anna giving the class a geography lesson. Anna was explaining that Siam was a very small country, even smaller than Britain. The King's eldest son had become angry with this and started shouting. The King had come to see what all the noise was about.

"Father! Father! Teacher say Siam small country. She say Siam even smaller than Englan'. This not true, is it,

Father? Father say Siam great country. *She* say Englan' better than Siam!"

"Teacher say WHAT?" yelled the King.

"Your majesty," said Miss Anna gently, "I never said Britain was a better country than Siam, merely that it was larger. Come and look on the map. You see…"

The King looked very scary and aggressive. He was a huge man with a completely bald head, wearing only a pair of loose, baggy pants that finished at the knee, and no shoes. He looked a bit primitive standing with his legs apart and his arms folded across each other.

"Silence, woman! Teacher wrong. Map wrong. Siam not small. Siam big. Siam biggest country in world! You disrespect king? Get down on your knees woman. GET DOWN ON FLOOR, NOW!"

Emma liked Miss Anna very much. She was pretty and had a lovely singing voice. Emma thought she was just the nicest lady that she had ever seen. She was like Cinderella, and Sleeping Beauty, and Belle out of *Beauty and the Beast*, all rolled into one. And if that big bully thought he was going to shout at *her* Miss Anna like that, and scare her half to death, well, he had another think coming. Emma had heard quite enough. She had become more annoyed as the King had shouted. How could he talk to her like that in front of all these people? If he wanted to tell her off he should have taken her away and done it quietly. And he was wrong too. The big ignoramus!

Emma had forgotten about the audience, apart from the fact that Miss Anna was being shouted at in front of them all. She had also forgotten about being shy. Emma was now a four foot high seething mass of anger, and the

King was going to get it. Emma had developed a strong and defensive hero worship of Anna.

She strode out from behind all the children and stood in front of the King. Imitating him, she parted her legs, and pointed her finger at his belly button.

"How dare you speak to Miss Anna like that, you… you…you…great big pot-bellied airbag! You say sorry to Miss Anna *right now.*"

"Wha…what?" the King spluttered. He looked confused, and glanced at Miss Anna. She just shrugged her shoulders to indicate that she hadn't a clue what was going on. The King looked into the wings where the director stood. He spread his hands and shrugged his shoulders, indicating that he didn't have clue what the little girl was doing either.

Emma wasn't finished yet, in fact, she was just getting going. She was a bright girl and although she could easily distinguish fantasy from reality she had become so completely engrossed in the unfolding of the story, and was so angry by the way the King was talking to her beloved Miss Anna, that she just momentarily lost herself. She forgot that it was only a theatre production.

"Of course Britain is bigger than Siam! Maps don't tell lies! So that makes you silly as well as bad mannered. And another thing," she went on, still wagging her finger at the King in anger, "Siam doesn't even *exist* anymore, so you even got the wrong map for your show. You'd think you would have got the right map, wouldn't you? Siam changed its name to Thailand years ago! And if you don't know that, well, that makes you more than just silly it makes you a …well, Mr King, sir, it makes you a dumb jackass!"

The King went red and one of his eyelids twitched violently as the curtain came down on the first act.

During the interval the children were herded into their dressing room to have their makeup touched up. They went past the King and the director, who were arguing in very raised voices in the corridor.

"How *dare* you change the script without telling me?" the King complained, now in a Cumbrian accent.

"Charlie, Charlie, I haven't. I knew as much about that as you did, but you have to admit the audience loved it. We'll keep it in."

The grown-up argument was soon lost in the cacophonous roar of the children's voices.

All too soon they were back on stage again. Miss Anna was giving the King a dancing lesson. The children were all on stage for this scene. The King and Anna twirled and sang to the song "Shall We Dance". They would sing, "Shall we dance, cha-cha-cha," and the children all had to stamp their feet in time to the "cha-cha-cha.

Mark was bored with all the dancing. He thought it was soft. As he stood on stage he began to sway from side to side, but not in time to the music at all. His arms swung out with each sideward movement in that way that only the arms of bored boys do. He looked up into the rafters of the stage and became totally distracted by all the lights and electrical rigging. Two men were up there, controlling the lights. Mark waved to them.

"Hiya! Don't fall down, will you?" he shouted.

One of the men looked as though he was going to do just that.

"Turn round and dance, you stupid kid," he hissed downwards.

Mark jolted out of his daydream. He realised that they were just coming to the stamp-stamp-stamp bit. He was good at that. Miss Anna and the King swished past him in their waltz just at that very moment, and Mark stamped hard on the King's foot three times.

The King sang, "Shall we dance, ow-OW-*OOWWW!*"

The audience roared.

Luckily, everything went quite smoothly for a while after that because the children weren't on stage much. The poor King had a terrible limp, though, and was obviously in a lot of pain. The audience just thought that it was part of the show and laughed every time he winced. When the children did troop back on stage it was at the state banquet that the King was giving for all the foreign dignitaries. The King wanted to show the people from England that they weren't a pack of "savage barbarians", and so the children had to present gifts to the visitors and say something nice to make the King sound like a wise and clever man. Not all the children had to do this, but they began to take their turn.

"Father, you clever man and velly wise."

"Father, you richest man in all Siam." The King frowned. "In all *world*," corrected the boy.

"Father, you velly best man in whole universe and best dancer."

Kerry was pushed forward. "Go on," said one of the wives, thrusting a carved box into her hand.

Kerry walked to the King and handed the box to him. But then she had no idea what to say. Feeling awkward as the silence went on she began to rock backwards and forwards.

"Psst!" it was the prompter. She was the lady who sat

in the wings and whispered the lines to any of the cast who had forgotten them. "Father, I wish you long life and lots of luck," she hissed to Kerry, thinking that Kerry had just forgotten her lines.

"Pardon?" shouted Kerry loudly, much to the delight of the audience. "Speak up, I can't hear you!"

"Father, I wish you long life and lots of luck," repeated the prompter, a little louder this time.

"Oh, okay," said Kerry, nonchalantly. "Father, I wish you would not limp like a duck."

Kerry didn't think the King looked very happy with her, and it took a long time for the audience to settle down.

*

It was almost the end of the show and the King was lying on his deathbed. His son sat beside him with his head lowered onto the counterpane. Sadly, the King drew one last, juddering breath and died. It was the most dramatic moment of the production. You could hear a pin drop. The cast loved the moment of shocked silence from the audience and held it for as long as they could...

Silence!

Well, silence that is except for a single, loud sob.

"Oh, no!" shouted Vicki, tears streaming down her face. She had two black lines running down her cheeks where the make-up had smudged. "That is just *too* sad!" she wailed, even louder. "He can't die. He's supposed to marry Miss Anna and live happily ever after." Vicki had become so involved with the story that she couldn't bear the thought of the King dying. She let out another loud sob, and ran right across the front of the stage, past the King's body, and exited stage left.

A muffled voice could be heard from the dead king under the blanket on the stage: "I…I don't believe it!"

The King moved slowly, until he was sitting bolt upright in the bed where he had just died. His cheeks looked purple beneath the brown makeup.

"I can't take any more of this," he spluttered in his Cumbrian accent. "I can't work with these…these… these…barbarians!" he added, borrowing a word from the show. The audience laughed and cheered. They loved the way the company had made the show even more of a comedy than it should have been.

The King got out of his bed and started to stomp off the stage in a terrible temper. Unfortunately, he got tangled up in the blanket and smacked loudly onto the stage floor. The unfortunate man twisted his already sore foot and howled in pain and humiliation. The audience laughed and laughed. They clapped long after the curtain went down. It took longer for everybody to take their places than usual because the director had to calm the irate King down, and it took a lot of persuasion to get him to go back on stage to take his bow.

The children in the show *always* got the loudest applause. They would join hands and go to the front of the stage in threes and fours. There they held their hands together and bowed deep. When Vicki, Emma, Mark, and Kerry went forward, the audience stood up to give them a standing ovation. They clapped and cheered and whistled and screamed. Emma's cheeks burned hot and red, but Vicki loved it and bowed not once but three times, until one of the stage hands shouted, "Oi! Gerroff!"

They leapt back with the strains of, Shall We Dance, ringing in their ears and smudges of greasepaint around their necks. It had been a fabulous night.

*

The first thing the children did when they got back to the bedroom was check the frame to see if they had broken the rule of not using it unwisely. More importantly, they were desperate to find out if a precious berry had been taken from them. They each breathed a huge sigh of relief when all the berries had been counted and twenty-three were all present and accounted for.

"Good night, Sylvia," they all said before moving away from the frame. They did that every night now, in case she was checking in on them through Granddaddy's clock face. Emma was the last to turn from the frame. She wasn't quite sure, but she was *almost* positive that as she turned, a wooden eyelid came down on one of the lizards in a quick, cheeky wink.

That night they all dreamed dreams of grease paint and spotlights. Vicki dramatically anounced that it was the best night of her whole entire life.

*

The next morning, Mr Taylor came to pick the four children up and give them a lift to school on his way to work.

"How was the show last night, Steve?" Nanna asked him.

"Ahh, it was brilliant," he said. "They did it really well. The kids were fantastic and they had things going wrong all over the place. I haven't laughed so much in ages. It really brought the show up to date. Some of the kids didn't half remind me of our four, though…"

Vicki, Emma, Kerry and Mark lowered their heads and ate their cereal without saying a word.

Chapter Seven
Hungry Eyes.

Although it was still summer, typical British weather was the order of the day and it was wet and drizzling. The kids had been cooped up all week and were going around the twist, so they had decided to go for a picnic.

Nanna had been told they were having a "video picnic". This meant a lunch of good things to eat and a big bottle of cherry cola while they sat and watched a couple of films in their bedroom. Normally, of course, the children weren't allowed to take food upstairs, but they had been complaining all day about being bored, so Nanna was more than happy to pack them up a really interesting picnic hamper if it kept them occupied for a couple of hours. While their grandparents thought they were safely sitting in their room watching videos, they were unlikely to be disturbed.

What they were really going to do was to leap into a wonderful picture of a forest glade for lunch. Emma had spotted the picture in a magazine and thought it would be a perfect place to visit. The others had been as impressed with it as she had. The trees had been cleverly painted. They parted to show a hazy mountain range, way off in the distance. The scene was focused on the mid-section of the picture, which featured a large clearing. A thick carpet of bluebells, hyacinths, late daffodils, and crocuses covered the grassy area like a dense, colourful carpet. Fallen leaves and pine needles softened the mass of deep blues, pinks, purples, yellows and greens and a shaft of strong sunlight speared through the trees to illuminate the scene. It was perfect. They had stuffed their reading books and sketchpads into the top of the hamper and were looking forward to a few hours of exploring and relaxing in the wonderful, enchanted forest. Kerry had reasoned that something *that* pretty just had to be enchanted. She was convinced that she would find a real live fairy to sketch, and, if not, then she would just draw the one that *would* come out to see them if it wasn't so shy. The others teased her and said that she was such a baby for believing in fairies, to which she turned on Mark and said, "Well, he believes in Dracula. How stupid is that?"

They held hands, Mark and Emma having one hand each on the hamper. Mark had reminded them all several times not to forget it, as if they could with him around. A picnic was one of his favourite things on earth.

Sand Lizard. Sand Lizard, cautiously creep.
Shim. Sham. Shally wham. Lizards leap!

*

The forest glade was everything that they had expected it to be. The densely covered trees lost their battle to keep the forceful sunlight out, making the spot cosy-warm. The flowers bowed their heads in greeting and the tree branches whispered to each other far above the four young visitors.

The children set about laying out their picnic. Mark hopped from one foot to the other, getting in everybody's way. Emma spread the yellow-and-orange checked tablecloth in a little area that was surrounded with gentle flowers. She was by far the most domesticated of the four and loved to play at being 'mother'. They found four rocks to hold the corners of the cloth down and stop it blowing away in the light, warm breeze. Then they dug into the hamper to find out what delicious goodies their nanna had packed for them. There were four sandwiches, each one cut into quarters so they could share the varieties: one each of ham and pickle, cheese and onion, tuna and sweetcorn mayonnaise, and, Mark's favourite, pork and stuffing with apple sauce. There were four sausage rolls, a packet of crisps each, some marshmallows and a huge slice of rich, dark chocolate cake.

"Blimey!" exclaimed Kerry, "there's enough here to feed an army."

"No, there isn't. We've got Mark with us," Vicki replied, grinning. Mark screwed up his face and threw a twig at her.

They began to eat. Of course, Mark ate all of his share and half of everybody else's. He sat munching happily, his cheeks bulging like a hamster and a look of sheer rapture on his stuffed face. As they tucked into their picnic, some little sparrows settled on the floor of the clearing, about ten or so feet away from them. The birds cocked their heads with hungry interest. The cousins threw some bread and pastry crumbs for them and laughed as the little birds fought and squabbled over the offerings.

Suddenly, the birds flew up into the air, cheeping loudly. The children looked around to see what had startled them, but there was nothing to see. *Something* had frightened the birds away, though.

They all sat quietly and listened for a few seconds. An unnatural silence fell over the forest. Something was out there. A distinct rustling in the undergrowth broke the silence. It came from the cover of the trees, somewhere to the left of them. A twig snapped loudly to their right, making them wheel around and peer between the trees. The noise told them that they were not alone.

The glade that had, just a few seconds before, seemed so friendly and welcoming to them suddenly turned sinister and dangerous. A wind stirred the trees. The leaves hissed, rustling together. Something was out there, hiding in the trees, watching them. They all felt it and drew closer together.

"What is it?" Kerry whispered. "I'm scared."

"It might be Dracula coming to suck our blood," whimpered Mark.

"I don't know what it is, but, there's more than one of them and they're coming closer," Vicki said, quietly.

The rustlings in the foliage continued. It was as if somebody, or something, was hiding in the trees all around them. The leaves seemed to be whispering: *"Danger, danger, danger…and there's no way out."*

"Let's leap," Kerry decided. "I want to get out of here."

They began hastily clearing the remains of the picnic into the hamper. Nanna would be furious if they lost it and they would have to think of an explanation for its disappearance from their bedroom.

Another rustling sounded in the trees, this time much closer. In fact, it was so close to Mark that he quickly slithered forward on his bottom towards the middle of the clearing. He turned to stare through the trees - to see if he could see anything. The hairs on his arms all rose as he heard a low, rumbling growl just a few feet in front of him. The thing, whatever it was, moved closer. He still couldn't make out anything more than a blur in the trees. He was aware of the size and shape of it. Whatever *it* was, *it* wasn't a human being, that was for sure.

Vicki scurried forward on her haunches, towards a large piece of broken branch that lay at the edge of the clearing. As she reached her arm towards it, she was sure that something was going to grab her and pull her right into the darkness of the forest. She picked up the branch without being attacked and moved towards Mark, who was the closest of the four children to the creeping thing that was coming towards them. The other lurking things had become still and silent. Vicki stood up and moved in front of Mark. She knew that if she was standing she would have a better chance of defending them all.

"Stand up, you lot," she hissed, "and stay close together."

"Be careful, Vicki," said Mark. "It's huge."

They had all shuffled back towards the farthest edge of the clearing. Whatever the thing was, it now stood just inside the trees. To get the picnic basket they would have to walk past it.

"Let's just grab the hamper and leap," Kerry said, crying now.

"We can't." Instinct told Vicki that if they moved within the line of the beast it would jump out of the shadows at them.

Another rustle as it moved a foot closer. The undergrowth parted. A pair of large, amber eyes glared coldly at them.

"Aaaagh, it's Dracula," screamed Mark, terrified.

"What is it?" Kerry shrieked, clinging to Emma.

"I dunno, Kez," Vicki said. "But whatever it is, it's big and it's mean, and I don't think it's a vampire."

The creature growled again. The sound was low, deep, a vibrating rumble that rattled in the animal's throat. It was, without a doubt, a threat. One wrong move and the beast would leap out at them.

All around the children grass and leaves rustled as the rest of the animals closed in on them. Soon, several pairs of eyes could be seen watching coldly through the trees. The yellow eyes stared at them in silent hatred. They were large, with pupils as black as oil in a well of amber, alert, intelligent eyes that didn't welcome visitors to their clearing. These animals had received no mercy in their lives and offered none in return.

The beast nearest Vicki and Mark was on the move again. The grass parted to make way for its hard grey chest to push through. The huge wolf stalked all the way out of the protective undergrowth. He stood five feet away from the children. They could smell the musky scent of his rough coat. He was the size of a large German shepherd dog, though slightly more lean. His chest bulged with muscle, his legs were firm and strong, braced and parted. He held his ground and made himself look as large as possible in front of the intruders. The hair had begun to rise from the centre of his back, a bristled ridge that extended over his shoulders and onto the back of his gigantic head. The cousins could not break away from the animal's iron gaze. Although he saw Vicki as the leader of this pack, his eyes bored into all four of them, keeping them rooted to the spot as he assessed his power and strength against theirs.

"Stand still and don't move. And, whatever you do, don't look away," Vicki said softly, under her breath.

"Couldn't look away if I wanted to," Emma whispered back. "But I think I'm about to wet my pants."

The wolf moved a step closer. Emma had to grab Kerry hard to stop her running. He had not stopped his low rumbling growl since he emerged from the trees. When Vicki didn't retreat as he moved that step closer, his lips pulled back in a snarl. His mouth dropped open. The vivid red of slaver-covered gums showed off his brilliant white teeth, perfectly. They looked like crystal icicles on a red velvet cushion. These teeth had been kept healthy by gnawing on the bones of its prey. Unlike lazy domestic dogs whose teeth become yellowed by eating prepared meal and canned meat the wolf's teeth had neither stain nor dirt on them. His snarl became more savage by the second. Spittle flew from his mouth. Several drops landed on Vicki, but she didn't flinch. She knew that no matter how scared they were, they must not show any weakness to the massive wolf.

Other wolves emerged from the cover of the trees, none as large as the big grey who had first challenged them, but big enough and mean enough and hungry-looking to boot.

"They probably just want the food," said Vicki. "I'm going to try and work my way around to the hamper to throw the food for them. Maybe then we can grab the basket and leap."

"Don't, Vicki!" Mark pleaded. "It's too dangerous!"

"Well, if we just stand here, sooner or later they're going to get fed up with just snarling at us."

"Aren't you scared?"

"Terrified! But I don't *think* they want to harm us. They just want to get to the food that they can smell."

Vicki inched one step sideways. The wolf snarled louder. He took a breath and rasped harder still, warning this challenger that the food was his, and he wasn't going to give it up without a fight.

Kerry did what Kerry always did in times of stress, she retreated into her brain and rummaged around in her memory for anything she could remember reading about wolves…

"They are Timber Wolves," she said, at last. "We are probably in Canada. That's where most of the wolves are, although they're also found in smaller numbers around the world. They won't attack us as long as we stay together. Well, unless they feel threatened or we back them into a corner."

"Er, Kez, I think it's us who are backed into a corner," Mark commented. "Maybe you could point this fact out to them and they'll go away like nice little doggies."

Vicki took another step to the side. This confused the wolf. His eyes shifted for the first time and he glanced between Vicki, the food hamper and the other three enemies who were near the rest of his pack. He was the alpha male, the lead wolf, it was his job to protect the rest of the pack. If they hadn't been so scared it would have been almost funny watching him trying to make a decision. Should he protect his pack from the intruders, or his lunch from the other pack leader? Deciding that his pack could look after themselves and that food was just too tempting to ignore, he snarled and moved another step towards Vicki. She moved one away. He moved two steps closer. She moved one out. This was all too much for him. He put his head back and howled.

The sound, so sudden in the stillness of the forest, sent icy shivers through each of the four children. It seemed as though the wolf was calling on the God of Wolves to come from the sky and aid him. While his head was up, brave Vicki used the opportunity to take another step. She was now completely separated from the other three and at her most vulnerable. The wolf came out of his howl and snarled with renewed viciousness.

Vicki had an idea. She began to sing in her softest, sweetest voice, "Michael row the boat ashore, hallelujah…"

She motioned for the others to join in. They began to sing, taking up the harmony and singing one octave higher, but just as softly as Vicki, so as not to startle the wolves, "Ha-le-lu-u-jah…"

That confused him. The Wolf flattened his ears and cocked his head to the side to listen. His snarl had subsided to a whimper, a soft rumble deep in his throat.

The children continued to sing and Vicki edged closer to the basket, very, very slowly. Once there, she knelt down and - never taking her eyes off the wolf – opened the hamper. She took out the remains of a sausage roll and threw it to the big grey wolf. He jumped backwards in surprise, with a yelp that he had the grace to look suitably ashamed of, then he moved forward slowly to sniff the offering. The other wolves came closer and Vicki threw what was left of all the food into the clearing. Then, while the wolves fought with each other over the scraps, she skirted round the edge of the clearing to get back to the others.

The largest female wolf chased off one of the young males who had stepped out of line in the pack order and tried to feed before his mother. She nipped him harshly on the flank to teach him some table manners and he ran off squealing. The clever wolf ran wide, going into the forest and circling around to come back on the other side of the pack.

He was only a few feet inside the tree line when a loud "*SNAP!*" echoed through the forest, reverberating eerily off the trees. There was a moment of total silence. All the wolves stopped eating, raised their heads, and pricked up their ears. The children listened, the birds listened and even the trees themselves seemed to calm and listen.

Suddenly, the most horrible howl resounded through the clearing. Something had happened to the running wolf. The sound was pitiful.

"Quick," Kerry hissed. "Let's leap."

"Kerry!" reprimanded Mark. "We can't. The poor animal's hurt. We have to try and help him."

"Are you crazy? What can we do? It's not as if he'll just let us go up and help, is it?"

"We have to try," Vicki said.

"We can't just leave him screaming like that," agreed Emma.

The other wolves were confused by the screaming pack-mate. They huddled together, not knowing what to do or where to go. Even the big alpha male looked uncertain. He howled in confusion.

The children made their way towards the sound of the wounded wolf. Vicki handed the big stick to Emma.

"Here," she ordered, "try and keep them back with this. They might attack if they think we are hurting the injured one."

Emma looked at the stick as though it was a marshmallow in a gun battle. "Gee, thanks, Vicki. I'm sure I'll do a great job with this," she replied sarcastically.

They pushed through some bushes and saw the young wolf lying at the edge of the path. His plight was only too obvious. He lay on his side panting, and at the same time howling in pain. As they watched, his head came up and he bit savagely at his hind leg, trying to free himself from the cruel jaws of a trapper's snare.

"Oh, no, the poor thing," Vicki cried, moving instantly towards him. Mark pulled her back.

"Wait a minute. We need to think about what to do. If you go near him, he's going to bite."

They stood looking down at the distressed animal, not knowing what to do to help him. The wolf was tiring quickly, his screams lessening and subsiding into whimpers with the odd yelp. He lay back down. His beaten body heaving with fear and pain as he panted harshly. His eyes were full of agony and terror as he turned to look at the four children gathered around him. Vicki felt sure that he knew that mankind had done this to him.

"What are we going to do?" wailed Vicki. Tears were streaming down her cheeks.

"Kerry, pass me the tablecloth," Mark said. "I have an idea."

Mark took the cloth and threw it over the wolf. The terrified animal grabbed the material and began shaking it savagely. He raged at the cloth in fury, snarling and spitting, punishing it for the pain he was suffering.

Mark flung himself down on top of the wolf and wrapped the loose end of the cloth twice around his snout. The rest of the cloth was over his head. This would help to calm the frightened animal when he stopped fighting.

Kerry screamed. The wolf was strong, despite being weakened and in shock. He fought and wrestled with Mark.

"Be careful, Mark!" yelled Emma.

"Hurry, Vicki! Open the snare. I can't hold him for long." Mark used the weight of his body to hold the wolf as steady as he could. The angry wolf bucked furiously, fighting against both the snare and the boy who had attacked him.

"Easy boy, take it easy, now. I'm not going to hurt you. We're going to try and help if we can. Easy lad. Easy." Mark softly spoke to the enraged animal. Gradually the fight went out of the wolf. He stopped struggling.

The other wolves had come to find out what was happening. They stood at some distance from the injured animal and looked on. None of them were growling and they didn't look as though they were going to attack, but all the same, they needed to be kept at bay.

Kerry very bravely moved towards them and waved her hands. She said things like "Shoo!" and "Go away wolves!" and "Please don't hurt us. We are only trying to help your friend." The wolves made no effort to move any closer. It was as if they knew that the children were trying to help.

Vicki tried to pry open the steel jaws of the snare but it was no good. She just wasn't strong enough. The snare held fast.

"Get the stick, Vicki, and try using that to get it open," Mark said.

Vicki prised the end of the branch between the snare's teeth and tried to force it open. The branch was rotten on the end and crumbled in the mouth of the snare. She tried again, and again it snapped. Every time she applied any pressure to the snare the wolf whimpered, and when the wolf wined, Vicki sobbed. He now lay completely still, not even trying to fight.

"It's no good. It won't work. I can't get it off. I'm not strong enough."

"Call for Sylvia," Emma said, a tinge of desperation in her voice.

"Of course!" Kerry enthused. "Sylvia! She'll know what to do."

Vicki stood up and grasped the lizard necklace. In a trembling voice, she chanted:

"Sylvia, Sylvia, calling you.
We're in the picture, come on through."

Despite the state of the injured wolf, Kerry couldn't help but snigger when Sylvia literally popped into the clearing in front of them. She looked very funny. She was wearing a bright orange leotard and a pair of black tights. She had trainers on her feet and a sweatband across her forehead. Her face was bright red, and her hair was plastered to her head with perspiration.

"Alright, alright. I know I look a sight. I was just in the middle of my 'Oldie & Easy' workout video. Now, what do you lot want that's so important you have to pull a woman out of her daily exercise routine?" Sylvia saw Mark and Vicki on the ground and summed up the situation in a second. "Oh my, the poor thing. Hold him steady, Mark, and I'll see if I can get this thing off."

She bent down and after a bit of huffing and puffing managed to release the trapped wolf. "Hold him now, while I have a look at him." She held the wolf's damaged leg and checked it from shoulder to paw.

"Well, he's a lucky fella," she began. "It doesn't look too bad at all. It doesn't even feel broken. If you lot hadn't been here, it would have been a lot worse for him. He would probably have bitten his own leg off to get free. Then the other pack members would have killed him. The winter is coming and they can't survive unless every pack member does his share of the hunting. It's survival of the fittest and the wolves know that. It would have been the end for this little guy. Good job you were here. Well done kids."

Sylvia moved the cloth to the side and checked him all over. He wasn't hurt anywhere else. She carefully unwrapped the cloth that was holding his mouth shut and frowned when he just lay still and made no attempt to move. His eyes were glazed, and, when she lifted his lip, she saw that the wolf's gums - which should have been bright red - were almost white.

"He's in shock, and although his leg isn't bad, there is a nasty cut on it that will be prone to infection if it isn't treated. I don't like this, but we have no choice. We have to take him back with us until he's healed. If we leave him here, he'll die."

The large female wolf came towards them and was pacing up and down a few feet in front of them. She was obviously distressed. She growled, low and soft.

"Don't worry, mamma. We'll take good care of him

and get him back to you just as soon as he's well enough." The female wolf cocked her head, listening to Sylvia's soft, calm tones. Maybe she even understood a little of what Sylvia was saying to her.

"Problem's going to be when we bring the little fella back. They might not accept him when he has the stink of human all over him."

Sylvia stood and picked the limp wolf up as though he weighed nothing at all. The animal wasn't unconscious but he was so exhausted and shocked that he put up no resistance. They all held hands, and Kerry held onto Sylvia's waist as she chanted them back to Brampton Hall.

*

Now, the cousins would have to be careful of the time. From the minute they stepped into Sylvia's house, they were on real time and not leap time. Sylvia told them to go before they were missed, but the children wouldn't hear of it until the wolf was settled.

"Are we going to take him to the vets?" Kerry asked.

"No, child, we can't risk doing that. Too many questions would be asked about where he came from. Don't worry, if we can bring him out of the shock, he'll be okay. He just needs to be kept warm and left to recover."

Sylvia bathed his paw in warm water and antiseptic. She smeared the wound in a healing cream and wrapped a bandage around it to stop the wolf licking all the cream off before it could do any good.

"Tomorrow we'll let him lick it better," she said. They put him in Sylvia's bedroom where it was warm and dark and pulled the door across so that he could be left in peace.

"Bye-bye Sylvia," the children said as they departed. Vicki had the last word, "We'll come back after tea to see how he is."

The children had no trouble sneaking in through the garage when they got back. Granddad had gone to take some rubbish to the tip and Nanna was watching Andre Agassi playing tennis. She was oblivious to everything but her good-looking hero.

They couldn't wait to get back to Sylvia's to see how the young wolf was doing.

Chapter Eight
Bad Lupus.

Every day, as soon as they were released from school, the children couldn't get home to change quickly enough. Once they had thrown themselves into their playing-out clothes and had hung up their school uniforms, they would tear up the hill to Sylvia's house to see the pup.

At first he was nervous and wary. He whined for the pack and was very unhappy, snarling at anybody who came near him. But, just two weeks later, you wouldn't think he was the same wolf.

They called him Lupus. Kerry thought of the name, she took it from the word 'lupine', which means *wolf-like*. It seemed to suit him and he quicly learned to come when he was called. But then, he would probably lollop over to whoever called, no matter what name they used. As the young wolf became tamer and tamer, Sylvia worried increasingly about him being reintroduced into the pack. She told the children that they must stop petting him. She might as well have asked them to stop breathing because Lupus had other ideas. He *insisted* on being petted and played with every second they were with him.

His wounds had healed well and he was soon fit and healthy, living on a diet of high protein dog food for "working dogs", supplemented with fresh raw steak. His muscles, which had previously been weak due to hunger and not enough food, became more pronounced by the day, until he was strong and wild and wilful…

He became the bane of Sylvia's life, the children would howl with laughter as Sylvia chased him around the room trying to retrieve one of her gaudy scarves, or a slipper, or the cushions from the sofa. One day they arrived to see Sylvia chasing Lupus through the garden. The wolf was grunting excitedly as he ran round and round the fountain trailing one of Sylvia's huge bras from his mouth.

"Get back here, you moth-eared lump of useless wolf! You just wait until I get hold of you, I'll beat you so hard I'll take all the skin off your rump and then fry it for my supper!" Sylvia yelled. But the children all knew she would never dream of harming a hair on the silly pup.

"Bring that back right now, or so help me, I'll turn you into an alley cat!" Lupus stopped mid-flight, ears pricked, tail erect, and for a second he seemed to consider the likelihood of this happening. His head went down and his bum went up, he quivered the entire length of his body with sheer pleasure at having invented such a "fun" game. Lupus growled deeply in mock-attack as he savaged the limp item of underwear. He shook his head and the mud-covered bra flew from side to side in his mouth, one cup resting momentarily on the top of his head like a strange, conical skullcap.

Sylvia puffed and panted as she drew closer to him. Her face was bright red and her eyes glinted with a mixture of exasperation and mirth. She bellowed a constant flow of threats at the delighted animal, who didn't believe a word she was saying. He stopped chewing and shaking the bra just long enough to grin up at the approaching ball of perspiration and colour that was plodding towards him.

He allowed Sylvia to get just ten feet from him, then he got that by-now-familiar look of pure, unrestrained mischief in his eye. He grabbed the bra back into his mouth and flew off down the garden with his prize blowing behind him in the wind. It was a trophy proclaiming his victory.

The children were doubled up in hysterics as they watched the strange performance being played out before them.

"Don't just stand there laughing, you pack of fools! Help me catch the rotten beast," Sylvia panted as she flew past. She was a blurred mass of red, yellow, blue, and purple. Her hat had slipped over one eye and her face perfectly matched the red of her silk Ali Baba trousers. It took the children several minutes to compose themselves enough to join in the chase.

It was almost too much for Lupus, who was in rapture. He led the five all over the garden, past bushes, around the rose beds and through the pond, much to the disgust of a surprised frog who croaked in shock. Who knows how long the spectacle would have continued if Lupus hadn't looked behind him to see how close they were, only to get his legs tangled in the straps of the huge bra. He tumbled ears over bum into an ungainly heap, rolled onto his back in submission and kicked at the white muddy lace with his strong hind legs. He grinned inanely and let his tongue loll out of the side of his mouth as the children piled on top of him.

"Oh, Lupus, you *are* funny! But you're a big pain!" said Mark happily. Lupus chuffed in agreement.

Lupus loved all the children, but he had formed a special friendship with Mark. Individually, the pair was bad enough…but together! Well, to coin one of Mark's favourite phrases, they were a big pain.

One day, Sylvia had been expecting the children at their usual time and had opened the door of the circular room in anticipation of their arrival. They had activated the secret door and were walking down the main tunnel to Sylvia's room when they saw Lupus coming towards them in the distance.

Mark was slightly ahead of the others and he bent over, slapping his hands loudly on his knees. "Lupus, c'mon, fella," he called. "Come here! Here, Lupus! That's right, good boy."

The wolf heard his beloved Mark and set off at an almighty pace down the tunnel. At first Mark was delighted, but then he realised the speed with which the wolf was pelting towards him. "Oh-oh, gangway!" he screamed, as he turned to run and collided with the girls. The corridor was too narrow; there was no escape.

The wolf got within ten feet of Mark and lunged. All four of his feet left the floor, and he whimpered with excitement as he landed heavily on poor Mark, who was thrown to the ground. Mark thrashed his head from side to side as Lupus stood over him, his front paws pinning the helpless boy to the floor. The cub licked him all over enthusiastically. Mark was powerless, unable to resist. Only when he was well and truly soggy and licked into total submission did Lupus move on to greet the rest of the children.

*

All too soon, the day arrived for Lupus to be returned to his own kind. There was no good reason to keep him any longer. Sylvia promised that he would still be there when they got home from school and that they would take him back into the picture together.

Mark had sobbed softly into his pillow the night before. He had grown to love the wolf, and, although he was happy to know that he was going back to where he belonged, his heart was breaking at the thought of losing his special friend. It didn't matter that he would be able to leap into the picture to visit the wolf. It just wouldn't be the same if he wasn't at the Hall every day when they got out of school.

All the children had heavy hearts as they stroked Lupus that afternoon. Sylvia clicked the lead to his black collar. She had to put it on him to keep him still while they leaped through the picture that the children had brought with them. Lupus wasn't at all sure about this strange thing around his neck and chewed naughtily at his lead. Sylvia was very worried that the other wolves would attack Lupus, what with him having been away from them for so long. They would be able to smell the human on him. It was a tense time of happiness at the thought of the wolf being back where he belonged and sadness at the thought of sending him home.

"Oh, come on now, you miserable lot. It isn't a funeral. We'll be able to go and see him sometimes. Personally, I'll be glad to see the back of the dratted thing," lied Sylvia with a tear in her eye. Lupus grinned up at his beloved foster mother and swished his tail.

*

When they leaped into the picture the clearing was still and subdued. The only sounds were those of the birds and the wind whispering through the trees. Lupus was excited and strained at the strange lead to be able to run to his pack. He had already scented them.

Sylvia couldn't just let him go without knowing if he would be accepted back in to the fold of the pack and it took all her strength to hold onto him.

She had found an enormous cooking pot in the Hall's kitchen and had made massive quantities of beef stew. Vicki and Mark set down the pot and took off the lid, releasing the smell of the rich gravy so that it whisped away through the forest to work its mouth-watering wonders…

After thirty seconds, Mark decided that they had waited long enough. "Oh well, it's perfectly obvious that they aren't coming. They've probably run south for the winter or somefink. There's nothin' else for it but to take him home with us again."

"Steady lad, they'll come," said Sylvia, with the authority of one who knows.

Sure enough, some minutes later the first crack of a breaking twig was heard downwind of them.

"They're here," Mark said, sadly.

"Aye, lad, be happy for Lupus. He needs his family more than he needs us, you know."

Big Grey thrust his way through the tall grasses and stood resplendent in the clearing. This time he was far more bold. After all, hadn't he won the battle for the food last time? These humans would surely think twice about challenging him again. He raised his head and gave a half-hearted rumble, warning the children that there could be trouble if they wanted it. Then he sniffed the air and a thick stream of saliva fell from his mouth to the grass at his feet. Emboldened by the heady smell of the bait, the other wolves came into the open. Big Grey moved to the pot and plunged his head into the depths of the beef stew. This was a sign for the rest of the pack to wade in and get what they could, while they could. Not one of them gave a second glance to Lupus.

Sylvia released the collar and without a backward glance he ran and stuck his head in the big cooking pot with his family. Soon, they had eaten all the stew and licked the pot clean. The wolves circled the clearing, looking for more food. When they had made sure that lunchtime was over, they turned their attention to Lupus, and his strange new smell.

His mother came forward slowly. This was her boy and yet she sensed that he was returned to her a different beast than that which had left. She circled him once, sniffing the air around him. Lupus instantly fell to the floor and offered his belly in a sign of submission. Mamma sniffed him all over, nudging him with her snout when she found a particularly strange aroma. The other wolves kept their distance.

Finally, Mamma nipped Lupus on the hind leg, as if to say, "Okay, I'll deal with cleaning you up later, you messy cub, but for now get up out of the mud and stop grovelling. It's unbecoming of a wolf of your stature and breeding."

The first and possibly greatest test was passed. Sylvia clutched Vicki's arm nervously as Big Grey moved forward. He sniffed the young wolf much the same as Mamma had done, though not as thoroughly. Again, Lupus dropped in submission and meek surrender, his tail quivering in terror of his imposing father.

The old wolf, perhaps giving thanks to the wolf spirit and protector flung back his head and howled. Soon Lupus was tumbling with his brothers and sisters, now that they had been given the all-clear to approach him.

The four adult wolves of the pack watched the adolescents playing for a few minutes and then Big Grey looked up at the sky. He found the Sun's position and sniffed the air. It was almost nightfall and time to move on. Letting out a small, authoritative bark, he brought the wolves into line. They instantly stopped their game and came to obedient attention.

Lupus looked at his father before flying back towards Sylvia and the children. He pranced and licked them all over... and then he was gone, tearing through the trees in hot pursuit of his brother, whose legs were just a little bit faster than his.

Mamma stood five feet from the humans. She hesitated, maybe wanting to move closer, but not daring, such a bad smell. "How could they smell like *that?*"

Her eyes met those of Sylvia - piercing, unnatural green eyes in tune with wild, amber ones. Two females locked in understanding. Mamma lowered her head and gave a small whimper that ended with her licking her chops. She swished her tail twice before reeling around to follow the rest of the pack that were already running for home.

"Well, that was a 'Lassie' moment and a half," said Emma, to Vicki and Mark, who were both sobbing unashamedly.

"You know, kids," Sylvia said. "I don't think our Lupus will ever forget us, especially if we bring the odd pan of stew for them all!" They all laughed, even Mark, who made quite a snotty mess laughing and crying at the same time.

*

Mark had driven everyone mad all morning going on about a competition on the Saturday morning children's show, "Get Up And Go".

His mum tried to explain to him that, yes, he was quite correct that the answer to the question was *Charlie and the Chocolate Factory*. But, she added, that didn't automatically mean that if he sent a postcard in that he would win the prize. But Mark had no doubt that this was a foregone conclusion. What did his mum know? She didn't even watch the program. *He knew the answer.* He really, really did. So, of course, that meant that he'd win the year's supply of free chocolate. His mum tried to patiently explain that a million other children the length and breadth of the country would also know the answer, would also send in a card, and would also be convinced that *they* were assured of the prize. But she knew that her voice fell on deaf ears. Mark was already sorting out some drawer space to house his hoard. The postcard was duly addressed and sent off to the programme. Only one week to wait until the winner was drawn.

That night Mark dreamed about the competition: *He was in the television studio to collect his prize* (in real life it would arrive by post), *and when his name was called he rushed forward as three hundred and sixty five yummy chocolate bars of every variety imaginable fell around him. He sank to his knees and began gorging on the wonderful icky chocolate. Manners had no place in such sweet dreams.*

Suddenly, a voice came over the microphone saying there

had been a mistake and that Mark hadn't been the only one who knew the answer and he had to share his prize with every child in the country...

It was terrible. It was a nightmare.

He woke suddenly, sitting up in bed sticky with sweat, the taste of the chocolate almost tangible in his mouth. He found it very hard to go back to sleep that night. What if he *didn't* win the precious prize? This was the first time that the possibility had seemed very real. He *was* going to win. Wasn't he?

The next morning he fretted constantly about the prize. He couldn't settle. Even winding his sister up didn't have its usual appeal. He had to *do* something.

That's when the first stirrings of an idea formed in his mind. He knew it was wrong. He knew he shouldn't do it, but who would know? He could always deny all knowledge.

Mark went round to his grandparents' house the night before the prize-winner's name was to be drawn on the pretence of picking up some schoolwork that he had left there. It only took a second to scribble out a quick note, put it in the frame, and chant the trigger verse. He felt butterflies of excitement in his tummy as the room gave a small jolt. Now, all he had to do was wait. Tomorrow his name would be drawn from the drum and he would win the prize.

The next morning they were all round at Nanna's watching the programme. Mark couldn't keep still. He was *so* excited.

"I bet you don't win it," Vicki said, in her best know-it-all voice that always wound her brother up.

"Oh, shut up, Vicki. I *am* going to win it, and when I do I won't be sharing it with you, so there."

"Mark, there is as much chance of you winning as there is of me being the next Queen of England," Emma said. "And that ain't never going to happen because Prince William's *much* too posh for me!"

"I am going to win, I am, I tell you, I know I am becau…" Mark trailed off and hung his head, suddenly realising what he had almost said.

"*How* exactly do you know you're going to win?" Kerry asked, already alerted by the way he had cut himself off mid-brag. She looked at him suspiciously. "What are you up to, Mark?"

"Nuffin', I just think I am going to win, that's all. And anyway, Emma, Prince William would never fancy you, because…because…you haven't got a tiara and you can't ride a horse!"

"I don't fancy him, anyway," Emma protested hurriedly.

"Sssshh!" Mark hissed, "this is it."

On the TV, the good-looking young man sitting on a bright yellow sofa with a huge cheesy grin plastered across his face was about to pick the name of the competition winner. Mark crossed his fingers on both hands. A knowing smile began to form on his mouth.

"*…And the winner is…Mark Forest, from Cumbria. Well done, Mark. The chocolate will be delivered to you in the next couple of days. Don't eat it all at once, now!*"

"YEEESSS! YEEESSS! It worked! It worked! I knew it wouldn't let me down!" Mark was flying around the living room with his hands in the air. The girls were sitting on the sofa with their mouths open.

Nanna came in from the kitchen to see what all the noise was about. "Well, well, well. You said all along you'd win. Do you have a magic wand or something?"

Kerry's eyes narrowed. She looked at her cousin suspiciously. She had a bad feeling about this. Following her hunch she went upstairs and into the bedroom. The frame sat on the mantelpiece as usual. It all looked in order from the doorway, but as she got closer she noticed a tiny red spot on the white paintwork of the fireplace. She knew what it was. Blackberry juice! Sure enough, one of the lizards had moved across the frame and was sitting close to the right hand bunch of berries. With a heavy heart Kerry began to count, but she already knew the total. As expected, one of the berries had disappeared. There were only twenty-two left. Each of the two bunches now had one berry missing.

"MARK!" she screamed at the top of her voice. Footsteps clattered loudly up the stairs, and the girls burst into the room to see what the matter was.

"Wazzup, Kez?" Vicki asked.

"Mark used the frame to win the prize!" Kerry fumed.

Vicki and Emma gasped.

"I did not," said Mark, who had slunk round the door looking very guilty. "That's a big fat lie." He had his hands in his pockets and his head down. His defence was not very convincing.

"Liar! One of the berries is missing. You know you did it and if you don't admit it I'm going to make you wish you had been born a slug. *Then* at least you could slither back under your dirty little stone."

"Awww, Mark, how could you?" Vicki said. "You

must have known we'd find out. You knew you were breaking the rules."

By now, Mark was looking most uncomfortable and was shuffling from foot to foot. There was no doubt about his guilt. "I thought it would be alright," he said lamely.

"Mark Forest, you would do anything for chocolate!" Emma raged furiously. "You'd even kiss bad breath Julie Smith if she'd just eaten a chocolate bar."

"Eurgh!" said Vicki and Kerry in unison.

"I would not." Mark managed to muster up a smidgen of indignation at this accusation. "Look, when the chocolate comes, I'll give you lot half of it."

"I don't think you should even have the prize," Vicki said, sternly. "After all, you only won it because you were dishonest."

Vicki sat on the bed with her hands resting on her chin and she began to hum to herself. This was a sign that she was thinking. After some seconds, she raised her head and the others stopped their ongoing argument to hear what she had to say. Mark instinctively knew that he wasn't going to like it.

"I think," Vicki began, in a voice that was clearly going to take no argument. "I think that you should give the chocolate to charity."

"*What?*" Mark spluttered. That was the most preposterous thing he'd ever heard. "Dream on, sister," he added. He'd heard that in a film and thought it sounded cool. "That isn't going to happen, and you can't make me."

Brave words indeed. Mark was painfully aware that Vicki probably *could* make him, but there was a lot at stake here, and he had to at least try. "I'm sorry, Vicki," he said, buckling at the thought of all that lovely chocolate being given away. "Please, let me keep it. I promise I'll do anything you say."

Vicki had made up her mind and she shook her head stubbornly.

"I know," Emma said, "there was that appeal on the radio yesterday for toys and things to be given to the children's hospital for the sick kids at Christmas. That would be *perfect*."

"No way," Mark said, in total disgust. "They'll probably be so ill that they'll only throw it back up again anyway, and that would just be a big waste. Oh don't make me give it away to a bunch of sick kids. You're just goody-two-shoes do-gooders and I'm not, so there."

"Did you know that in this country alone, over three thousand children spend Christmas in hospital?" droned Kerry matter-of-factly.

"Did *you* know," droned Emma, imitating Kerry, "that in this country alone, one irritating girl is going to get thrown out of a bedroom window for being a super nerd?"

"You are *going* to give the prize to the hospital. RIGHT?" ordered Vicki, beginning to lose her temper.

"No," Mark said. The thought of ten Chinese burns was better than the thought of losing three hundred and sixty-five chocolate bars.

Vicki got a pen and paper and began to write.

"What's that? What are you doing?" asked Mark, in a small, worried voice.

"Oh, it's just a note to put in the frame, asking it to make you vomit every time you eat one of those chocolate bars. I can't make you give them away, but I *can* make sure that you don't enjoy them."

"Oh, alright then! I'll give it to the rotten kids in the rotten hospital!" Mark knew when he was beaten.

"Hang on," Emma said, "If he gives all that chocolate to the hospital, he's going to be a flippin' hero. That's not fair, is it?"

"Hmmm, hadn't thought of that," Vicki mused. "He'll just have to donate it anonymously. We'll get Mum to drop it off next time she goes into town."

The chocolate duly arrived the very next day. And Mark *was* a hero, even if it was only his parents and grandparents who thought so. His mum had a tear in her eye when he told her he wanted to donate his prize to the hospital. Vicki nearly choked when she saw them all flapping around him, she was that angry.

"Oh, Sweetie, you are the kindest, gentlest, most generous lad in the world. I am *sooo* proud of you," said their mum.

Mark beamed with this burst of praise, until he saw Vicki's face glowering at him behind his mother's back.

"We-ell, Mum, to be honest, it was all our Vicki's idea," he said truthfully.

Both the children had been given five pounds for being so thoughtful. They decided to share it with their cousins and they all had lunch out at the Happy Kids Eatery.

"It's nice to think of all those kids having some chocolate on Christmas morning," said Mark, happily munching on his Super Burger with double cheese and extra fries. "I'm glad I gave it to them. They are giving away computer systems on this week's 'Get Up And Go', maybe I'm on a roll!" He smiled sweetly at the girls as a large glob of mayo dropped onto his chin.

"*Eurgh*, gross!" Vicki said, suddenly losing her appetite.

Chapter Nine
Kaleidoscope Castle.

The children sat looking at the colourful picture of the castle. It was *amazing*. They were in no doubt that this was going to be an interesting leap. Mark had come across the picture in a fantasy tales book. At first glance, it appeared to be an ordinary view of the front face of a medieval castle, but when you looked closer, things didn't seem quite right...

"Let's do it!" exclaimed Vicki, jumping up and down on the bed with excitement.

They gathered around the frame and joined hands. Their leaps so far had been strange and adventurous but somehow they just knew that this one was going to be different from all that had gone before:

"*Sand Lizard. Sand Lizard, cautiously creep.
Shim. Sham. Shally wham. Lizards leap!*"

*

When the world finally settled they found themselves standing on the lowered drawbridge of a magnificent castle.

"Wow," Mark said, "this is brilliant! I wonder if it's a real castle with knights and kings and swords and stuff?

Maybe we'll get caught in the middle of some big battle and get to shoot the catapults at the enemy!"

Kerry looked around in awe. "Or maybe we'll meet Guinevere and Sir Lancelot."

"And if we're really, really lucky, we'll get to drink tea out of little china teacups with the Mad Hatter and Alice and the Knights of the Round Table," added Emma, sarcastically. "It's not *that* kind of castle, stupid."

"And how do you know, miss know-it-all? You always think you're so clever with your sarky remarks and comments. This is magic, Emma. Anything can happen. One day you might even think before you speak." Kerry was on the point of slipping into her customary huff, brought on by Emma taking the mickey out of her.

"Pack it in, you two," Vicki ordered. "This is supposed to be fun, remember? If you are just going to argue, you might as well go back home and do it." Then she looked up at the castle. "Should we pull on that big rope, do you think?"

A long rope hung at the side of the drawbridge with a little sign beside it saying, "Here ye pulle."

"What are we going to say if someone answers?" Vicki wondered.

"Oh, well, Kerry can ask for King Arthur and the white rabbit Emma said with a smirk. Kerry glared at her.

"I'll pull it. Can I? Please, can I be the one to pull it?" Mark spat on his palms and rubbed them together, much to the disgust of the girls. Then he moved towards the rope.

"AAAAAAAAAAAA-CHOOOO!!"

Vicki yelped. Emma jumped. Kerry grabbed Mark,

and Mark nearly fell in the water filled moat, dragging Kerry with him.

"What on earth was that?" Vicki's voice trembled, and they all looked around for the phantom sneezer. Nobody was in sight.

"AA-CHOO! Well, you lot were at the back of the queue when they were giving out brains, weren't you? Up here, Einsteins."

They glanced up to find themselves looking into a pair of lively bright blue eyes. What the children couldn't quite come to terms with was the face that surrounded those eyes. All the features – eyes included - belonged to a gargoyle. A rather ugly stone face carved into the rock of the castle wall. This was a female gargoyle with tendrils of stone hair and a chipped rock face.

"Boo!" said the gargoyle, rather unconvincingly.

"Boo yourself", said Mark, who, after spending several months jumping through a

picture into goodness knows what, found that he was not in the least bit frightened.

The gargoyle was taken aback by the boy's boldness. "I said '*Boo*'. You are *supposed* to be scared."

"Why?" Mark asked.

"Well, you just are, that's all. It's the nature of things. I say 'boo', you get scared. Been that way for hundreds of years. Don't see why you should think you can just come along and change things. What are you trying to do? I suppose you want my job, don't you? You've got the face for it. Just because I'm old they think they can throw me in the quarry and replace me with a new-fangled modern-type gargoyle. Well, I'm not going, I tell you. I've been here eight hundred years and I'm not done yet!"

Mark sighed. "Okay, okay," he said kindly. "Let's try it again, and we'll see what we can do."

The gargoyle smiled, revealing stone gums and no teeth. She took a deep breath, puffed her cheeks up, and said "BOO!" in her most intimidating voice - which Mark secretly thought wasn't very intimidating at all. In fact, he was quite positive that he could do much better. Nevertheless, the four children screamed, and the gargoyle grinned with gummy pleasure and pride. "There now, that's better. See? I'm good for a few hundred years yet!"

Vicki giggled. "You're funny. I like you."

The gargoyle's grey cheeks went pink with pleasure. "Hey, GC, wake up! Hear that? This young 'un likes me. GC, WAKE *UP*!"

A few feet away, and parallel to the female gargoyle, a pair of brown eyes opened in the brick; a male gargoyle snorted as he woke up. "Wha..? What is it, woman?" He sounded very angry. "For eight hundred years I've been trying to grab forty winks, and every time I get to twenty-three, *you* wake me up. Now, what is it this time? Cramp in your jaw again?"

"Oh, shut up moaning, you old boulder. We've got company. Look," said the female face.

"I know, I know. I'm tired, not senile. Listening to your nagging for centuries would make anyone weary. Now, who have we here and what do you want? I am the Great Cobble, honourable right gargoyle of Kaleidoscope Castle. That there's the missus, the not-so-honourable left gargoyle. She's called Stone Cladding. I call her Og, or Old Granite. You can call her Og as well, everybody does."

GC found this incredibly funny, and lapsed into gales of laughter.

"Well! You chiseled old lump of nutty slack …," Og began.

"Oh, be quiet, you bucket of sloppy cement dust."

Mark was enjoying this argument very much. The others didn't quite know what to do to stop the warring gargoyles. This fight had probably been going on for some time.

"Ahem. Excuse me, Mr GC? May we come in, please?" asked Kerry, politely, while attempting to acquire that 'butter-wouldn't-melt' look, which usually got her her own way.

The gargoyles stopped fighting mid-sentence and stared down, open-mouthed, at the cousins.

"*Come in*?!" bellowed Og. "You can't just *come in* to a castle like this. There is a certain protocol to be observed, you know."

"Well, what do we have to do?" enquired Kerry.

"*Well*, if you don't know *that* you'll never get in, will you? It's obvious. You have to solve the puzzle. The more puzzles you solve, the deeper you can go into the castle," said Og. "It's simple."

"Where do we find the first puzzle then?" asked Mark, eager to begin the quest.

"Should we tell them, Og?" GC wondered. Og nodded her head and grinned. "Okay, listen carefully because I'm too tired to be repeating myself. Ready?"

The children all nodded their heads. This was exciting, they liked puzzles.

"Okay…combine the number of crocks to the rocks,

add seasoning and remove flower. Yank the hank and if the number's right, apply hope to the rope."

"What?" said Kerry, annoyed. "That doesn't make sense. What do you mean?"

"That's the clue kid, take it or leave it." GC muttered, obviously bored with this interruption and eager to settle back into his slumber.

After some time, they were no closer to a solution than when they first sat on the drawbridge to ponder the problem. What made thinking even more difficult was the regular and monotonous snoring from GC that resembled an elephant in agony.

"Oh, I'm fed up," said Vicki, who had very little patience. "This is stupid. What does it mean? All those cooking pots and rocks and salt 'n' pepper and flour. And does he mean plain or self-raising flour? It makes all the difference, you know. I never was any good at cooking. How are we supposed to know the recipe, or what to do with it? It's dumb."

"Okay," Emma said. "Let's go through it again. Crocks and rocks. What do you think that means?"

"It could be something to do with crocodiles," Kerry offered.

"Oh, at *last*," came a grumpy voice behind them. "I thought you were never going to get there." Og eyed GC suspiciously to make sure he really was asleep, and then whispered to the children, "I'm not supposed to give you any clues, but try calling the crocs by name."

"What are their names?" Kerry asked, innocently.

"Oh, don't you even know *that*?" Og sounded exasperated. "Are all human children as slow as you lot, or are you exceptions to your species? Well, if it's the only way to get rid of you and get some peace…," she lowered her voice. "Try calling 'Tick' and 'Tock'."

"Well," said Emma. "We know that there are two of them, so we don't need to bother calling them do we? Let's go on to the next part. Combine crocks to roc-"

"I want to see them!" yelled Mark excitedly. He ran over to the guard-rail and peered down into the moat. "Tick!" he called, "Tock!" Nothing happened. The others joined Mark and called for the crocodiles.

Suddenly, there was an enormous splash directly behind them. For the second time Mark almost fell into the moat in shock; only this time the others nearly toppled over the guard-rail too. They wheeled round and there, with their scaly grey snouts on the drawbridge, were the two vicious looking crocodiles.

"Nice one, Mark. What do you do for an encore?" Emma said dryly.

Kerry, who had a passion for anything reptilian, was enthralled and gasped in wonder. The other three gasped in sheer terror and pressed hard into the rail, shuffling their feet as far back and away from those protruding teeth as it was possible to get without landing in the moat with the crocodiles.

"We are going to die," whispered Vicki, theatrically.

"Don't be so stupid," Og said. "They'd have eaten you by now if they were going to. They want you to stroke their snouts."

"Hang on just one second here," Emma said. "Now, I know you think we're stupid, but there *are* differing degrees of stupidity and we are way down the ladder from stroking children-eating crocodiles."

"Wow!" Mark began. "This is the best thing ever,

stroking a real live croc. I can't wait to have grandkids to tell them this one." He was already down on his knees and moving slowly towards the nearest croc. He stretched out his hand and the crocodile blinked. His hand moved back to his side a lot faster than it had moved out. "Well, maybe I won't bother just now, after all. Not that I'm scared or anything. I just don't want to get my hand wet." He put his trembling hand back into his pocket and tried to appear unconcerned. But, whistling and swaying from side to side, he fooled nobody.

Kerry knelt down beside him and put her hand firmly on the animal's long nose and began to rub it. The croc tilted his head into her hand. Soon, all four of the children - even Mark the Brave - were stroking Tick and Tock. The children were convinced that the crocodiles were grinning from ear to ear. Well, they would have been had they had any ears. Eventually the crocs grew bored with the game, and, as if there had been some sign, flipped back into the water. They sped off, swimming very fast, and did a furious lap of the huge moat. Half a minute later they approached from the other side of the bridge and in perfect synchronisation flipped their strong tails in the water, sending a huge wave of spray over the four children. It was just like being at Seaworld, well, a Seaworld populated with crocodiles. The children laughed and waved goodbye to their new friends as the crocs swam away into the deeper, cooler waters of the moat.

"Okay," said Emma, getting back to the puzzle. "Add the crocs to the rocks. Rocks? Rocks? What can that mean? Can you see any rocks anywhere?"

"Ahem," coughed Og, pointedly.

"Sshhh, please, Og," Vicki said, "we're trying to think."

"Of course!" Kerry realised. "Og. It's the gargoyles. Add the crocks to the rocks. So, two crocks and two gargoyles. That makes four. What's next?"

"Add seasoning," Emma remembered, "something to do with salt and pepper?"

"Not necessarily. What if it's something to do with the seasons?" pondered Kerry.

"The four seasons!" yelled Mark. "Four and four is eight. Remove flour. Well, remove could be minus. Minus flour. What do you think it means?"

"Dunno," Vicki shrugged. They sat down again and continued to think. This wasn't as easy as it had at first seemed.

"Psst!" said a little voice from above. "Whistle to the windows."

"What do you mean, whistle to the windows?" Mark asked.

They all stood and whistled as loudly as they could. Movement in some of the narrow castle windows caught their eye. As they looked more closely they saw three plastic flowers in three different windows. They were the kind that danced when you made a noise. As the children whistled, the little plastic flowers, in their little plastic pots, danced gaily, doing their little plastic dance with big yellow smiles painted on their brown faces. What a strange mix of ancient and modern this castle seemed to be!

"Three flowers!" chanted the four children in unison.

"Eight minus three is five," Kerry said. "We've got the answer. It's five. We have to ring the bell-pull five times."

The children jumped up and down and hugged each other with excitement.

Unfortunately, all the noise had woken up GC .

"Now, what's going on? Is it one of them there new-fangled football matches where you kick a pig's stomach around the place? We never had hooligans in the days of the gladiators, you know. Twenty-three winks, if only I could reach twenty-four," he sighed, wistfully. "Are you lot still here? You make more noise than a battalion of Scots charging the castle in kilts."

"I'm sorry we woke you again, GC," Vicki said. "We've solved the clue and we're going to ring the bell five times now."

Mark began to pull the rope. Somewhere, far away, a cock crowed five raucous crows in time to the rope. Then the portcullis rose on its chains and the huge castle door opened, leading onto a cobbled courtyard.

"Bye, GC! Bye, Og!" the children shouted as they went through the massive oak door. "It was nice meeting you. Hope to see you again soon."

The gargoyles laughed loudly. "Hah! GC, they think they are going to come out again. Do you know, in eight hundred and twenty years nobody has ever come back out of that door?" The children turned around nervously, but it was too late. The door was almost shut behind them.

"Oh, hold your tongue, womannnn…" GC said, falling asleep on the last word and beginning to snore soundly.

*

The children stared in fascination at the array of colour and nonsense before them. Emma loved mathematics and was particularly interested in the shape of the courtyard. She couldn't make any sort of logical order out of it. The yard was in the shape of a huge square, or maybe it was a circle, for it had no corners. Yes, it *was* a circle. But on the other hand it *did* have four sides, so it *couldn't* be a circle. It was a square because four rows of castle buildings made up the four edges. But as her eyes travelled upwards, Emma noticed that the walls had a sort of inward curling shape that smoothed out all the angles. Perhaps it *was* a circle, after all.

"Is this courtyard a square or a circle?" she asked the others, who were still staring round in disbelief.

A woman dressed in a green tunic and tights ran past them very fast. She had a quiver full of arrows on her back. "Neither," she answered, obviously having heard Emma's question. "It's a Squircle. If you see Floss would you tell her that her horrible dragon has been in my bed again?"

"Er…yes, of course," Emma replied, as the lady disappeared through a door in the far wall of the castle. "But who's Floss?" she shouted after the woman. It was too late, the lady had gone.

Vicki and Kerry were staring - and Mark was giggling - at a colourful fire-eater off to the left of them who had blown a cloud of flame out of his mouth and had set fire to his hands. He jumped up and down making "Oooh! Oooh! Oooh!" noises. Then he bent over and placed his hands between his knees to try and quash the flames. This only served to set his loose trousers on fire as well. Running across the courtyard, he jumped in the trough of water set against the wall opposite the children and let out a huge sigh of relief as spirals of smoke rose around him. Mark thought the poor man's misfortune was hilarious and laughed until tears sprang from his eyes.

"Are you alright?" asked Vicki, in a concerned voice as she ran over to the man sitting waist deep in the trough of water.

"Aye, lass, aye. It was a good day today. Yesterday it was my face." He looked up, and Vicki tried very hard not to laugh as she saw that the man only had one bushy eyebrow and half a moustache. This set Mark off on a new fit of laughter. The man looked across at him, astonished. He frowned for a moment, and then he too set off laughing. The sound of the two of them howling rang across the courtyard and echoed back. It was some time before they managed to stop. The man held out a dripping though seemingly unharmed hand to Mark, who helped pull him out of the trough.

"Thanks, lad, I'm Galileo, the fire eater, and you are?"

"Mark Forest. This is my sister, Vicki," he said, "and these are my two cousins, Kerry and Emma. It's very nice to meet you. I hope you don't set fire to yourself again."

The man assured them that he would do his best not to and set off in search of something called "strong mead". Mark thought this was a person, but Kerry explained that it was an alcoholic drink. Kerry always knew odd stuff.

A lady in a long black skirt and red jacket, with a three cornered hat on her head, had walked into the centre of the Squircle. She honked a black bicycle horn three times, and shouted "Oyez!" a lot more than three times. People gathered around her. "Oyez! Oyez! Oyez!" she shouted, very loudly some more. Mark was impressed and gazed at her in awe.

"Get on with it, Marcella," drawled an impatient man near the front. "What's happening?"

"Oyez, Oyez, Oyez, good King Luke has decreed that Kaleidoscope Castle is in trouble with the King's officers. He has not paid his taxes to himself for years. If the castle fortune isn't recovered soon, the castle itself will fall into disrepair and everybody will perish and die."

The crowd groaned loudly. "Gerroff," said the rude man at the front of the crowd. "It's the same old message every single week. Can't we have some new news? It's ages since we had anyone hung, drawn and quartered. And when was the last case of dysentery? We haven't had a single Holy War since we got the new court seamstress, and swine fever is down by a third since chef got her recipe for pork medallions. Every week it's just the same old message. Nobody will ever solve the last puzzle, and the King's fortune will remain locked away forever. Get off your soapbox, woman, and make me some food!" After his tirade, the man threw a rotten tomato, which hit the town crier in the face.

"I'll get you, Jamar," she said. "You just wait till I get you home tonight, I'll be serving you bread and drippings for a week. And don't think Chef will feed you. Since she caught you stealing her gooseberries last week she's had a cleaver sharpened with your name on it!"

The crowd roared with laughter and the little man hung his head and shuffled off. Everybody seemed to be moving through the large double doors in the wall opposite the drawbridge. The people seemed disappointed that the town crier's news hadn't been more exciting The children were standing by the well in the centre of the Squircle, trying to decide if they should follow, when from another door a tall lady appeared. The four gaped in astonishment as they saw her dragging two huge, green, scaly dragons behind her.

The smaller of the two dragons seemed of the opinion that he had walked far enough and eased his big bottom down onto the floor. The lady pulled and pulled on his lead, but he would *not* be led.

"Kevin, this is *not* funny. Stand up right this second or I'll dose you with kerosene, and next time you breathe out, you'll go up in a puff of smoke."

At the mention of the word 'puff', the other dragon put his snout firmly into the lady's tummy and pushed lovingly. The woman was lifted clean off her feet and dangled in mid-air for a couple of seconds on the dragon's nose.

"Oh, Puff," she said. "I wasn't talking about you, boy."

The children walked over to the woman while keeping a healthy distance from the extraordinary looking dragons. "Erm...excuse me please, are you Floss?" asked Vicki, tentatively.

"Yes, girlie, I am. I don't suppose you four could get behind Kevin and give him a good shove, please? He can be so stubborn sometimes. I'm taking them for a B-A-T-H." Floss spelled out the word and Kevin trembled visibly. "What was it you wanted, anyway?"

"Er...we saw a lady dressed in green, and she said to tell you that your horr...er, that one of your dragons had been in her bed. I don't think she was very pleased."

Kevin, the smaller of the two green dragons, grinned sheepishly as only a young dragon can. He rolled his eyes, trying his level best to look innocent. He would even have gone so far as to whistle nonchalantly, but every time he tried that he singed something.

"Oh, Kev," Floss said, in a tone of deep disappointment. "Have you been in Ratchet's bed again? She's going to be in a horrible temper when she comes back. You'd better get your bath and then find somewhere to hide, and I don't mean in Ratchet's bed because she's going to come looking for you."

Floss moved off across the courtyard with the two dragons in tow. Thankfully, Kevin saw the error of his ways and decided to move away quite willingly, so the need to push from behind was not necessary.

The main door to the castle was still open. "I wonder if we can go in?" Mark asked. "There is nobody here to set us a puzzle."

They walked to the door, and just as they were about to go through, a large grid fell down before them. A little man stepped out from behind a huge potted yucca plant that looked almost as out of place there as he did.

"What's the password?" said the little gnome-like man. He spoke in a high-pitched, wizened voice and looked most peculiar. He wore a suit of green and red silk and a funny little hat in the same material with three bells on it. His face was thin and pointy, and he had two big red circles painted on his cheeks.

"I said, *what's the password?*" repeated the little man, growing impatient and jumping from one foot to the other.

"Er…I don't know, sir," said Kerry politely. "What *is* the password?"

The funny little man was flummoxed. "Well, it's… well, it's…well, I don't know what it is. I'm just supposed to set you a puzzle. I say, I say, I say," continued the man. "What do you call a man who runs backwards with his tail between his legs?"

"Very odd, I should think," Emma replied. "Where we come from men don't usually *have* tails."

The man walked over to Emma on his bandy legs and gazed up. His tiny, piggy eyes were jet black. He looked her up and down and seemed unimpressed with what he saw. "Hmm, a fellow jester, eh? Where's your suit? You don't honestly think you look funny like that, do you?"

"Not nearly as funny as you do," Emma said. The jester smiled happily at what he thought was a compliment. He stood on his tiptoes and shook his head three times in Emma's face. His hat bells tinkled. "See? *This* is what a jester is supposed to look like. Where are your bells?"

"Do you know, I was just asking my three friends here the same thing. Where are my bells? I said. One minute there they were sitting on my head like Big Ben in triplicate, and then *poof,* they'd vanished. I think *we* should be setting *you* the task of finding my missing bells."

The little man looked positively terrified by this suggestion. "Oh, miss, I'm only poor old Canticlee the jester. I can't be going off solving puzzles. My brain isn't made that way. Knock, knock?"

"Who's there?" said the four in unison.

"Password."

"Password who?"

"Pass word to old Canticlee that you want to come in, and he'll let you."

"Can we come in, please, dear Canticlee?" Vicki asked, sweetly.

"Of course you can. Don't know why you didn't just ask me in the first place. I'll be sure to bring your bells, miss, if I find them."

"Thank you," Emma said, as they passed through the lifted grid. "And I'll think of some of my best jokes for you. By the way, what do you call a jester without bells?"

"I don't know?" Canticlee replied. "What *do* you call a jester without bells?"

"A blessing!" she shouted, running through the door.

Their last view of Canticlee was of him mouthing the words "a blessing" several times, and then frowning as he stood scratching his head and looking puzzled. He decided that mortal's just weren't cut out to be jesters.

The children found themselves in an enormous hall. It was cool, and Kerry shivered under her thin cardigan. The hall was the size of a football pitch. It was quite dark, but not at all gloomy. The place looked ancient, but what the children couldn't understand was the odd modern conveniences strewn around the place. As they entered, to the left of them stood an old electric cooker. It would have looked out of place in a castle anyway, but to find it in the Great Hall beside the door was even more odd. The floor was laid with the most spectacular mosaic. Hundreds of thousands of hours work must have gone into creating it. The walls were hung with luxurious tapestries and stuffed animal heads, instruments and weapons, portraits, and… a large poster of Sylvester Stallone as Rambo!

A girl of about Emma's age ran up to them. "Hello, I'm Tour Guide Barbie. Who are you?"

The children looked at each other and tried very hard not to smirk at the friendly, though decidedly odd girl.

"Action Man, Cindy and Tiny Tears…," began Emma, pointing to each of the others in turn.

"Stop it, Em," Vicki ordered. "I'm Vicki," she said to the other girl. "What's your real name?"

Just at that moment a door was flung open at the other side of the room, and what could only be described as a wizard came hurtling through it.

"Amyrillis? Amyrillis?" he shouted, as he bore down on the girl.

"Ahh! There you are, child. I've been looking everywhere for you. Have you mixed the wasp stripe and the caterpillar curl with the willow wisps yet? You know King Luke has that boil on his…er, oh yes, behind his ear, isn't it? He's been in pain with it for three days now, and if I don't mix something soothing he's going to be declaring war on the Hegots again. You know how much trouble that caused last time. Poor Queen Careela was picking thorns from her cushion for weeks."

"Oh, Uncle, do I have to? You know how hairy those caterpillar curls are."

"Child, if you want to be a great sorceress one day, then you have to learn the craft now."

The wizard looked down with pride on his pretty apprentice, and the family resemblance was apparent. He was a kind-looking man with a round face and warm brown eyes that twinkled as he spoke. He wore a sort of purple dress with sun, moon, and star pictures on it and the customary pointed hat. He was a fine wizard and looked just like the ones in all the good storybooks. He even had the long white beard.

"And who have we here?" he boomed, looking down and smiling on the children. "Visitors, how nice, we don't get many visitors here. I am Simian the wizard and this is my niece Amyrillis," he announced, holding out his hand to each of them in turn.

Kerry stifled a giggle, and Mark turned to look at her. "Simian means monkey-like," she offered by way of explanation. Mark snorted and Simian turned to them grinning, his sharp pointed ears having caught the conversation.

"Aaahh," he said. "But I am not the only monkey here. No doubt you will meet Monkey in due course. He is an orang-utan who escaped from cruel owners who were going to turn him into a curry. He is highly intelligent and loves to meet new people. We are very proud of him. I expect he's either watching videos or is sitting in the library reading."

Mark jumped up and down in excitement. "Can we go and see him now?"

"Well, I don't think you can do that, my friend. Not without solving a puzzle first."

"What is the puzzle, please?" asked Mark, who could hardly contain himself.

"Oh, I don't know. I expect someone will be along before too long to tell you. Now, if you'll excuse us, Amyrillis and I have some work to do."

The wizard and his trainee sorceress walked away, Amyrillis pulled a face behind her uncle's back, then she grabbed his hand lovingly and off they went to mix their potions and spells.

The children were left alone. They wandered around looking at what must have been priceless antiques. Two full suits of armour stood in opposite corners of the room. Mark couldn't resist lifting the visor on the one nearest to him. This was Mark's nature. If there was a sign saying 'wet paint' by a wall, Mark would have to run his fingers along the wall to see if it really *was* wet. If you were polite, you would call him 'naturally inquisitive.' He approached the armour and lifted the metal visor.

"Hello," said a gruff voice from within. "What can I do for you, young man?" They should all have been used to things jumping out at them by this time, appearing from nowhere and just generally popping up or out. Nevertheless, Mark sprang three feet into the air. The visor clanged shut, noisily reverberating around the echoey hall. The knight raised a creaky arm and opened it again.

"I'm Ernest the white knight, and my counterpart over there is Adam, the black knight."

Adam raised his arm in greeting.

"I don't know," said Mark. "Knights and kings, all we need now are some prawns and we can have a game of chess."

"Pawns, dear cousin, pawns, if we had prawns we'd have a Chinese takeaway, not a game of chess," Emma said. Too late, she realised what she had said.

"I'm hungry," Mark whined.

"Can you tell us the next puzzle, please, Ernest?" asked Vicki.

"Ooh, I couldn't do that, little Missy. More than my job's worth. I dare say Lidlia will be along soon. She'd be the best person to ask." With that, Ernest cocked his creaky arm and looked at his gold watch. He signalled to Adam in the far corner, and they began to move out towards the courtyard.

So many people were coming and going, but nobody here actually seemed to *do* very much…

Marcella the castle crier came in at that moment and took off her hat, her jacket, and her boots. "Be a darling," she said to Mark, "and put these on the coat, hat, and boot stand, would you, please?"

Mark looked around but could find nowhere to hang the clothes.

"Oh, Silly me," Marcella said. "Of course, you being visitors and not being used to our grand ways here, you won't have seen a posh coat, hat, and boot stand like ours before, will you?" She walked across the room, and, while the kids stood in open- mouthed astonishment - not for the first time that day - she explained: "You see, you put your hat on this darling little curly ring here, and then you open the door and put your boots in here. And then you hang your coat on the knobs at the side there. Never use the proper coat knobs, though, because there is something wrong with the stand. He doesn't like it when you hang your coats on the proper coat knobs, so the castle carpenter had to fix some special ones to the side. Before, every time we hung our coats on his knobs he got angry and burned all our hats."

It was no good. They tried. They really, really *did* try to keep straight faces and not laugh at the nice lady with the loud voice, but it was no good. It was bad enough when she put her hat on the burner, but when she opened the door and put her boots in the oven it was all too much for the kids. By the time she explained about the 'coat, hat, and boot' stand getting angry and burning their hats, the children were howling. The coat, hat, and boot stand was, of course, the electric cooker!

Marcella decided there was something very wrong with these visitors and ran off to tell Jamar of the terrible laughing sickness the strangers had brought into the castle.

The next thing that happened was very peculiar. A door opened and about half a dozen very large ladies walked through it. They were all dressed identically in long brown dresses with aprons covered in big pink flowers over the top. They had slippers on their feet and shuffled along rather than walked. They each wore a hairnet, with a scarf tied into a knot on the top of their heads. Three curlers stuck out of each lady's scarf and lined up on her forehead.

"Well, I sez to 'im, I sez, you can't treat 'er like that. And do you know what he sez back?"

"No, Nellie, what did 'e say back to 'er?"

"'E sez…"

The ladies walked across the room, still gossiping avidly, seemingly totally oblivious to the four children. One of the women walked to the far wall and switched on a vacuum cleaner. The children couldn't believe their eyes. The cleaner was a huge orange cylinder-type vacuum with a smiley face on the front. Its brush had been removed to reveal the open hose. The cylinder itself was standing with the hose attached to the wall so that it ran like a chimney from the cleaner. The women shuffled slowly across the room, bending down and picking up tiny pieces of rubbish and litter from the floor; then they would shuffle back with each one and deposit it in the vacuum cleaner pipe.

"Are they mad?" asked Kerry, in a hushed tone.

"Totally nuts," affirmed Emma, "loopy, wacko, round the twist."

The women finished their 'vacuuming', turned off the cleaner, and shuffled back out, all the time keeping up their constant stream of gossip.

The cousins were still giggling to themselves when another lady bustled towards them. Whereas the cleaning ladies had shuffled, this one bristled with brisk efficiency.

"Aaah, there you all are. I was told we had guests. Have you solved the puzzle yet, then?"

"Oh, dear, no, we haven't," Kerry said. "We don't even know it yet."

"Young lady, how *dare* you come into this castle using such foul language? That will be one golden groat, please." The lady pursed her lips and looked down on Kerry angrily while holding her hand out expectantly.

"Oh, dear," Kerry said again, flustered. "I think you misheard me. I said that we hadn't been told the puzzle. I never said anything naughty."

The stern woman gasped. "There you go again! See? Swearing. That'll be two groats, please. Does your mother know you talk like that?"

Kerry looked at the ground. She was confused and had no idea what she'd done wrong. She had a horrible feeling that she was going to cry.

"Listen here, love," Vicki began, in her most grown-up voice.

"Oh, there you go *again*, three golden groats, please."

"I don't understand. What have we done wrong, and

what are golden groats anyway? We certainly don't have any," Emma said.

The lady reached into her pocket, which gave every impression of being bottomless. She drew from it an enormous scroll. Clearing her throat, she began to read in a self-important voice, "Rule seven hundred and sixty-three of the Kaleidoscope Castle charter clearly states: 'Anyone heard to utter any terms of endearment will be charged an on-the-spot fine of one golden groat'." She finished reading and rolled the scroll back up before returning it to her pocket. Next, she drew from the same pocket an enormous calculator. Without turning it on she pressed the number two once. "Two of those plus one of those," she pressed the number one, "makes, er…," she counted on her fingers, almost causing her to drop the calculator. "Er…yes, that's right. Three golden groats, to be paid immediately or you will be thrown into the castle dungeons for all of eternity."

She put the calculator back in her pocket and once again held out her hand, awaiting payment.

"Hang on a minute," said Emma, "I don't remember uttering any terms of endearment. Do you three?" The others shook their heads solemnly. They didn't quite know what Emma was doing, but they knew she was up to something. "Would you mind telling us exactly what we said wrong, please?"

The lady looked right and left to make sure that nobody was within earshot. "We-ell," she said, reluctantly. "The first girl said 'dear' twice, and the other one said 'love'."

"I'm sorry," said Emma sweetly, "but I didn't quite hear what you said."

"They said 'dear,' twice, and 'love,' once," the woman said, a little louder.

"Oh, I see," pondered Emma, slowly. "Well, by *my* reckoning, *you* have just said both of those forbidden words twice. So, if you deduct the three golden groats we owe you that surely leaves a balance of one golden groat owing to us. Still, I think we could just agree to say no more about it, don't you?"

The woman went pink as Emma's trickery sunk in. But, instead of being angry as they expected she might be, she smiled broadly. "Well, you're clever. I'll give you that. My name is Lidlia. I am the castle treasurer, appointed by Good King Luke to save the castle from ruin. It's my job to collect as many golden groats as possible to give to the King. The people here are so gentle and loving that the best way we could think of to do this was to fine people for the use of loving words. Nobody minds, really, because everybody wants to save the castle. Maybe one day someone will solve the final puzzle. Anyway, talking of puzzles, I suppose you would like to know what the next one is?"

"Oh, yes, please," said the four children, with a mixture of trepidation and excitement.

"Okay. Well, you have to bring the bear to life and make him sound the bugle. See? Easy, I'm surprised that nobody has managed to do it in the last eight hundred years, it's so simple."

"Do you know how to do it, then?" asked Mark, in awe of the formidable lady.

"Er…well, actually…um…no," she replied. "But if it was *my* puzzle I'm sure I could soon work it out."

The children moved into a huddle to discuss the

problem. The bear in question was obviously the bearskin rug, with its head still attached, that lay in front of the huge fireplace, and the bugle was hanging on the wall.

It didn't take the children long to work the problem out. Mark was taking this puzzle, and he walked into the centre of the room, feeling very important. He had a very special role to play and went grandly over to the bearskin rug and shrugged it over his shoulders. He was now inside the bearskin, and so it looked as if it had been brought to life. He walked over to the bugle and reached up to take it from the wall so that he could blow it.

"Ah-ah-ah," warned Lidlia, "I'm sorry, children. Did I forget to mention that you are *not* allowed to be touching either the bearskin or the bugle when it is played?"

"She knows flippin' well that she did," grumbled Emma. "The old-" she looked round and saw a moose's head on another part of the wall, "moose!" she finished. The children went back to their huddle and thought some more. They thought until their heads ached. They thought until their tummies ached, which was particularly upsetting for poor Mark, and they thought until their brains ached.

Some time later, Lidlia took pity on them and brought out a lovely afternoon tea from the castle kitchens. Chef had cooked a ham especially in honour of the new guests. At differing points the children leaped back home to keep the grandparents off their backs, and to buy themselves more time, though, in reality, only half an hour real time had gone past at home while they were in the castle.

After what seemed like an age, the cleaning ladies once again trooped into the hall and repeated their vacuuming ritual. The children watched distractedly, but Kerry sat bolt upright and stared at them intently. Her eyes became alert and her brow furrowed, as it did when she was on the point of making some important breakthrough in one of her science problems. Vicki knew that look. Kerry was on the point of coming up with something. They all felt a stirring of excitement.

The ladies shuffled out again.

"Got it!" yelled Kerry. "Come on, you lot, help me, please."

They dragged the vacuum cleaner over to the bearskin. Then they carefully took a broadsword from the wall. It was very sharp and Lidlia helped them to position it firmly on top of the vacuum cylinder. They fastened the vacuum hose along the length of the sword so that the opening of the hose stopped just at the top of the sword. They placed the bearskin on top of the sword and positioned the hose so that the end of the pipe just showed from the bear's mouth. The teeth were helpful in securing the pipe in place. Then they set the bugle into the end of the hose, resting the end of it on a Queen Anne chair so that it was supported in the bear's mouth. Finally, the children turned on the vacuum cleaner and stood back to watch.

For a few seconds nothing happened, and even Lidlia's face fell. But then, deep resonant sounds blew loud and clear from the end of the bugle. The bear had come to life, and, while he may not have been playing the morning salute, he was certainly making a noise. The children clapped and cheered. Everybody hugged everybody else. Even Lidlia was caught up in the excitement.

She led the cousins proudly through to the library. These were her protégés. Nobody had ever got farther than the Great Hall before. This was a first. Rumours were flying around the castle about the children and people were staring at them intently. Some said that the four children had a rare madness that would spread through the castle and kill them all. Others said that they were great visionaries from another time who knew everything there was to know. Some people were saying that these four children had come to solve the final puzzle.

At the far end of the library, away from all the gas lamps, some people were sitting huddled in the corner reading. "Here we go again," Emma said, "loony tunes time."

"Oh," said Lidlia, "I see you've noticed our Caleptic lighting. We are very proud of it, and it is a great Castle honour to be given a turn to read by its magic light." Four men were sitting in thick coats with books on their knees. They shivered occasionally.

"Unfortunately," continued Lidlia, "the Caleptic lighting has a very strange magic. We don't understand why it gets so cold when you open the door to turn it on. Still, it's only a minor problem. Simian, our wizard, is working on a spell that will give us the Caleptic lighting without the cold. We think that the Caleptic lighting box has been cursed by a wicked witch at some time. Simian is a powerful wizard and will find a counter-spell."

The children giggled as they walked away from the people huddled round the fridge. Nothing surprised them anymore, a medieval castle with electricity? Talking gargoyles? Reading apes? This was bizarre.

"Oh," said Vicki suddenly, as they turned around and saw the orang-utan sitting at one of the tables with a book in his hand.

The creature was startled and hid behind his book making little whimpering noises.

"That's Monkey," Lidlia said. "He's very shy. You see, when he was with the cruel people they used to poke him and tell him that he was very ugly. Now he believes that he is."

"Oh no!" Vicki exclaimed, "he's *beautiful*. Please put the book down, Monkey, so that we can come and talk to you."

Slowly, slowly, the ape lowered the book, and a pair of intelligent brown eyes peered over the top at the four children. He had a big face with a nose that looked as soft as velvet and lots of long silvery red hair. But his eyes looked sad.

"I hate those people for what they did to you," Vicki said angrily. "If I got hold of them I'd stick electrodes on their heads and fry them up into brain toast. You are beautiful, Monkey, and we love you." Vicki was known for getting passionate about animals.

"What are you reading?" asked Mark matter-of-factly as though it was the most normal thing in the world to ask a monkey what his preferred literature consisted of. Monkey relaxed visibly, grateful to the boy. Reading was his passion. He loved books and spent many happy hours in the castle library reading up on everything he could find. Of course, he couldn't speak, that would just be silly but he turned the book over and pointed to the title to show Mark that he understood his question and that he was happy to respond.

"*A Tale Of Two Cities*," said Kerry. "Wow, Monkey! That's some pretty intense reading."

"Actually," said Lidlia, "the next puzzle concerns

169

Monkey. He has been making mad gestures for weeks, and we can't understand what he's trying to tell us. It's obviously something very important to him. We have been through hundreds of books looking for pictures that would give us a clue, but have come up with nothing. If you can find out what it is he wants, that will take you to the final puzzle, the *all-important* final puzzle, the puzzle that, once solved, will save Kaleidoscope Castle."

The children felt very important. This puzzle was the easiest to solve of all so far. It only took them two minutes and a little kindness.

When Lidlia walked back into the room, Monkey sported two beautiful hairslides - one above each eye - donated by Vicki and Kerry. Every time he had tried to read, his hair had fallen into his eyes. All he wanted was something to tie it back. He was very proud of his new slides and turned this way and that, looking in the little vanity mirror that Vicki held for him. They all agreed that he looked very handsome, and Vicki didn't have the heart to take the mirror off him, so she let him keep it. As they left the room, Monkey had his head buried in his book, but every few seconds he stopped to look at himself in the little mirror.

It was announced that after some light refreshments, the children were to be presented to Good King Luke himself to be given the final puzzle. They felt a little bit nervous, but very excited at the same time.

In the kitchen they met the Chef. She was standing in the centre of an enormous kitchen, turning a spit with a whole pig roasting on it.

"Oh my," she said, "I wish there was a quicker way to do this. Lookee here, it's almost time to eat and I haven't even got the pig roasted yet. My arms are killing me. I've been turning this thing for four hours and it's still not cooked through."

"It must be very boring doing that all day," said Kerry.

"Oh no, not really, King Luke is very good to me, you see? The last time I threatened to poison his food with arsenic he provided me with my very own entertainment system. Look." She pointed to the corner of the kitchen where goldfish swam happily behind the portal door of a huge *microwave oven*!

"Shall we tell her?" Kerry asked.

"Nah," said Emma. "She's happy, bless her. And, anyway, we have a King to meet."

Chapter Ten
Of Keys Kings And Treasure

Lidlia burst into the kitchen where the children were still talking to Dawn, the chef. She licked her finger and wiped a smudge of chocolate cream from Mark's chin. He rumpled his face in disgust and tried to fight against her, but it was no good, she had wiped too many chocolatey faces in her time to be defeated by one small boy.

"Gerroff!" Mark said, ungraciously.

"Okay, you'll do. Good King Luke has summoned you. He is free to see you right away. Follow me."

It seemed they walked down endless corridors before they came to a large wooden door that said, "Ye olde throne roome". Lidlia threw open the door grandly and announced the children.

"The four amazing puzzle solvers, your Majesty." She bowed low and edged backwards out of the door.

"Come, come." A rather high-pitched voice floated towards them. "Steppest thou this way, that mine eyes might rest upon thee."

The children began the walk up the red carpet. The throne was at the end of a very, very long room. As they got their first look at King Luke they were more than a little surprised. He was no older than they were, a boy of only maybe twelve or thirteen years old.

"Hail, travelers," he said, discarding the toy Porsche car that he had been "driving" with his royal fingers up and down the arm of the great red velvet throne. "Hast thou come to retrieve my assets?"

Vicki and Kerry curtsied low and gracefully before him. Mark hopped from foot to foot, and Emma stood and stared at the little boy in the big chair.

"Eh? What did he say?" Mark asked, looking puzzled.

"He said," Emma began, "'Hast thou…' Oh heck, I think he means, have we come to get his money back for him."

The King hid a grin beneath his arm. His tunic sleeve was long enough, and loose enough, and white-ruffed enough to hide not only his grin, but most of the rest of him as well.

"Where is your money?" asked Emma, "and why can't you get it yourself?"

"Oh, Milady. It hast been under lock and key for many ages. Mine serfs hath been driven down by the score. Mine knights hath failed me. Mine gladiators hath perished. Many hath tried to gain entry to the golden room, but all hath been stricken down."

"What's he saying?" Mark was even more confused now.

"I think he's got a lisp, bless him," Emma said.

"I said," sighed King Luke, now sounding just like any other boy who had decided to drop his "thees" and "thous". "My treasure's all locked up and everyone who has tried to get to it has been killed by either the crocodiles or the Floor of a Thousand Spikes."

"Well, I don't know why you didn't just say that in

the first place," Emma said. "We might have understood you."

"And now," King Luke continued, "you have come from another land to release my treasure and save the castle from ruin-"

"Now, wait just a second there, your worship!" Emma interrupted.

"Majesty!" cut in Vicki, importantly.

"Whatever," Emma said. "You say everybody else who has tried has been killed? Well, I'm so sorry not to be of any assistance, but, you see, I'm only ten, and although they don't know it yet, my grandchildren are planning a big eightieth birthday party for me."

Now, it was the young king's turn to look puzzled.

"Just ignore her," Vicki said to the King. "She thinks she's funny. Her mum should never have bought her that joke book for Christmas, she hasn't been the same since."

"Are you saying you won't help me? But you *are* the four amazing puzzle solvers."

"Ahh, but…you see, there is a big difference. Solving puzzles has not so far been life threatening. This final puzzle sounds a little more complex and dangerous. And, anyway, I couldn't possibly deny my father the pleasure of paying my way through college."

The King's face had fallen. His smile was gone. His bottom lip had protruded and was in danger of hitting the floor with a "thunk!" In short, Good King Luke was sulking. His golden, bejewelled crown - which was, to say the least, too big and probably too heavy for his head to support - had fallen over one eye. He tried to stamp the floor in temper, but as his legs were two feet off solid ground and dangling in mid-air, this just made him look all the more silly.

He clapped his hands twice and shouted loudly, "Guards!"

Four men appeared from two doors, one at either side of the throne. They looked very funny with their knobbly knees and bright red tights.

"Guards, take these four prisoners and throw them in the dungeons immediately."

Kerry looked around in horror. She raised a hand as one of the guards approached to grab her. "Don't touch me. Don't you *dare* touch me!" she screamed. The King nodded his head to let her have her say. She stomped up the three steps towards the King, and Luke shrank back in his throne slightly as he saw the look of fury on her face.

"Go, Kez," whispered Vicki.

Kerry's long blonde pigtails bounced up and down furiously as her head bobbed in anger. "Prisoners? *Prisoners?*" she shrieked. "I thought we were guests. Do you treat everybody like this? I thought you looked very nice when we came in, but now I can see you're just a rotten bully. Good King Luke indeed. I think you are *Bad* King Luke, and if you were *my* King…well, I'd rather have Henry the Eighth, and he was bad too because he chopped his wives' heads off, and there were a heck of a lot of wives, too."

"Who is this Henry the Eighth?" asked King Luke.

"Oh, he hasn't been born yet. But if he *is* ever born here, you'll be sorry. If you just asked us nicely to help you, maybe we could see if there was anything we could do, without putting ourselves in danger. But when you threaten to have us thrown in the dungeons…well, it's not very friendly, is it?"

King Luke hung his head in shame. "I'm sorry. Will you help us, *please*? Without the treasure we have no money to pay the workers, and the castle needs repair, and my mother and father are sick, and the crops are dying, and-"

"All right, all right," Kerry interrupted, softening a little. "We get the idea. Well, we can't promise anything. But it wouldn't hurt to talk your problem through with you and see if anything can be done."

King Luke visibly cheered up and sent the guards away, but only after demanding that they brought chocolate fudge sundaes for everybody. This pleased Mark especially, and he was more than happy to try and help in any way that he could.

Kerry helped King Luke down from the massive throne, and they all went to sit around a little table overlooking the Squircle to eat their desserts and talk.

"Well," said King Luke through a mouthful of chocolate sauce and ice-cream. Kerry thought this was rather bad manners while Mark thoroughly approved of it, but was not allowed to do it. "The final puzzle is in two parts. Firstly, you have to get the Golden Key - that opens the Golden Door to the Golden Room - and then…,"

"And will we find the golden goose who laid the golden egg? And all live in golden happiness ever after?" asked Emma, who was beginning to find all this hard going.

"And the second bit?" asked Vicki, ignoring Emma.

She noted a certain reluctance on the King's part to elaborate.

"We-ell," Luke sounded even less sure of himself. "Then all you have to do is run the gauntlet of the Hall of Death and open the Golden Door with the Golden Key. See? It's not so difficult, really."

"What is the Hall of Death?" Kerry asked, a tremor in her voice.

"It's a bit difficult to describe, really," said the King evasively. "Best that I show you if you're not dea ... If you get that far."

"And the Key?" Kerry persisted.

"Oh, that's easy," King Luke proclaimed, in a voice that rang with false joviality. "It's just at the bottom of the moat. You see, many years ago, when Good King Mephistopheles came back from the crusades with one thousand chests of treasure, he locked it all in the Golden Room for safekeeping. *Then,* he booby-trapped the hall outside the Golden Room. *Then* he set up the controls so that they could only be turned off from *inside* the Golden Room. *Then* he threw the key in the moat where it would be guarded by the moat crocodiles. *Then* he forgot that he couldn't get back in when he needed to pay the milkman. Hence the castle has been failing ever since and milk has been scarce."

Vicki stifled a giggle. "That was a silly thing to do."

"Yes," pondered King Luke. "His wife must have thought so, especially."

"Why's that, then?" Mark asked.

"Well, he forgot she was still in the Golden Room when he set off the booby traps."

"Oh!" the children gasped, with suitable solemnity.

"Ha ha! Only joking," King Luke laughed. "She was so angry that she couldn't get to the treasure she put him in the castle stocks and ordered everyone to throw rotten fruit at him for a month."

"That's awful," Vicki said. "Did he die?"

"No. He just grew very fond of soggy tomatoes."

"Well," said Mark, after he had licked his tongue round the inside of his sundae glass. "I think we should take a vote on whether or not we can help."

"I have an idea for retrieving the key," Kerry said.

"And I have an idea for running the gauntlet," added Mark proudly.

"All in favour of trying say, 'Aye'. Can we pull out of it if we can't do it?" Kerry asked.

"Er, yes," said King Luke, doubtfully.

"You promise, now?" Kerry did not completely trust his word.

"Cross my heart and hope to die, I'll even spit in a dead dog's eye." This seemed to satisfy the four amazing puzzle solvers.

"Aye!" Mark said, loudly.

"Aye," Emma said, confidently.

"Aye," Vicki said, quietly.

"Aye," whispered Kerry, tremulously.

King Luke leaped from his seat. "Come on, then! Let's get started!" He was very excited and walked off in the direction of the moat.

Something had been bothering Kerry since they arrived at the castle, and while they were walking to the drawbridge it seemed the ideal time to ask him about it. "King Luke? You live in a medieval castle, and yet you have electricity and modern cookers and things. Where do they come from?"

"Oh, you mean the antiques? Well, they were left behind by our ancestors, who lived in a more advanced age. Do you know they even had horseless carriages? Good grief, these days we don't even have the carriages, never mind the horses."

"What are horseless carriages?" asked Vicki.

"He means cars," Kerry said. "That's what they used to call them in the old days."

"No, no, girl," King Luke said. "That was long ago in the *new* days, hundreds of years ago, when people flew across the sky in big metal birds, and had things called computers that took over the world. We are far more civilised now. One day in the future, man will even undiscover fire." King Luke shook his head in wonder, as if this was something awesome and amazing.

"Wow!" Kerry exclaimed. "This world is going backwards as ours is going forwards. It's amazing!"

They were still letting the reality of this crazy world sink in when they reached the drawbridge. King Luke peered over into the murky water; instantly, the crocs appeared. They weren't going to let anybody get near that precious key. Tick licked his lips greedily; he had learned that whenever somebody tried to get the key, lunch followed very quickly.

"Right," said Kerry. "Mark, I need you to leap home and get some stuff that we will need." She reeled off a list of things that he should collect. "Oh, and look in on Nanna and Granddad to buy us some more time, please."

No sooner had Mark gone than he leaped back again,

for time was a funny thing. He landed right in front of them on the drawbridge and nearly knocked Good King Luke off balance. As they gathered around him, he laid out all the articles that he had brought from home. Luke's eyes widened with curiosity; he hadn't seen any of these odd things before.

Kerry started the proceedings. "Mark and Vicki, you go and call the crocs at the other side of the moat and stroke them for five minutes. If they swim off, whistle to let us know."

The two crocodiles - who had just minutes before been hungry predators - turned into lap-crocs as they were called out of the water for some petting time. As before, they twisted their heads so that the children could stroke behind their ears. It didn't seem to occur to the crocodiles that these were the same beings that tasted good if they landed in the water.

At the other side of the moat, Kerry got to work quickly. She didn't have a lot of time before Tick and Tock got bored with their new friends. She assembled Mark's fishing rod rapidly, working out which section fitted into which. The reel gave her some trouble, as she had never used one before; but soon the rod was threaded and ready for use. Instead of hooking the line and baiting it, Kerry attached a nine-inch magnet to the end. She was ready to go fishing.

King Luke was mesmerised as Kerry fed the line into the water, watching the magnet sink lower and lower until it became lost in silt and mud at the bottom of the moat. They waited for a few minutes for the water to clear, and then she very slowly moved the magnet towards the large iron key. Kerry felt a slight tug as the key attached itself to the magnet, and she began to reel in the line. She wound the reel slowly at first, and then a little faster. Suddenly, the line went loose and she groaned as she realised that the key had fallen back to the bottom of the moat.

"Oh, me! *ME*!" gasped King Luke, jumping up and down excitedly, "my turn. I demand a turn, by order of the King. I demand a turn at fooshing."

"Fishing!" Kerry shouted, exasperated. "You *are* rude. No, you can't have a go because I've caught the key again." This time she reeled the line in more carefully Very, very slowly, she turned the reel handle as gently as possible so that the key didn't jolt off the magnet. Luke was sulking again, but soon brightened up as the slimy green key appeared out of the water. He jumped up and down and clapped his hands just as a shrill whistle came to them from the other side of the moat. Five seconds later the two ferocious crocodiles were snapping at the hands that, sadly for them, were just out of reach.

"We've got it, we've got it!" shouted Kerry, excitedly, as the others ran up to them. "We've got the golden key!"

King Luke was more interested in the concept of 'fooshing'. Mark said that Luke could borrow his fishing rod for a couple of weeks so that the castle Maker could make something similar. He also promised that before they left he would show the King how to bait the line with fresh juicy worms so that they could catch some fresh fish for supper. King Luke was delighted. He was also easily distracted and was far more interested in "fooshing" now than continuing with the final puzzle. The children, however, were riding high on their initial success and were keen to see if Mark's idea would also be successful for the second part. They had to force King Luke to put the fishing rod down and virtually dragged him back into the castle. Their enthusiasm was to be short-lived!

King Luke unlocked a security door that kept hapless explorers away from the Hall of a Thousand Spikes, or the Hall of Death, as it was otherwise known. The children stood at the threshold of the perfectly ordinary - though extremely long-looking - corridor.

"Doesn't look so scary to me," said Mark scornfully.

"No?" King Luke asked.

"Uh-uh," Mark added, acting brave.

Luke took a shiny red apple out of his pocket. He very slowly polished it on his tunic, confiding in the children that ermine fur makes a wonderful apple polisher.

Emma was about to say that fur belongs on beautiful animals not ugly Kings, but, knowing how King Luke was prone to both sulking and throwing people willy-nilly into the dungeons, she thought better of it.

King Luke took a huge bite out of the apple and chewed slowly, enjoying being the centre of attention and taking his time to make his point. Mark was just about to ask for a bite of the juicy apple when Luke bowled it over-arm down the hall. It sailed through the air for several seconds before coming to land about halfway down the long corridor. The children giggled when nothing whatsoever happened.

"Maybe the spikes seized up!" laughed Mark.

King Luke just shrugged his shoulders and stood with his hands in his pockets.

Suddenly, an earth-cracking blast came from the ground beneath their feet and froze the very laughter on their lips. One thousand ten-inch spikes rose in a split second, littering the hall floor and gleaming in pointed splendour. The apple was impaled upon a spike halfway down the floor. After about a minute, in which nobody said a word, the mechanism below them cranked into action and the spikes lowered back beneath the ground. The apple plonked onto the smooth floor, cut into two perfectly symmetrical halves.

"No way!" Vicki cried. "No way are you going down that hall! I'm your older sister, and I'm not having it! You are not going to be a boy of two halves."

"Agreed," Emma added. Kerry just looked as though she was about to faint.

"I can do it, sis," said Mark. "I know I can. Look how long it took for the spikes to come up. It must have been about thirty seconds. Nobody could *run* down that corridor in time, but on a skateboard it'll be a doddle."

"It's too risky. You are *not* doing it."

"I know I can do it. There's just enough time if I get a good kick-off."

"And if you don't?" Emma asked, looking at the halved apple.

"I will. I'm good."

"Let me do it," Vicki offered, bravely, but she shook so hard as she said it that she'd have had trouble getting *on* the skateboard, never mind "running the gauntlet", as the race down the Hall of Death was known.

Mark studied the smooth floor. It was ideal for boarding. If God and a bit of luck were with him, he would have enough time to get down the corridor and up onto the Golden Doorstep to safety before the spikes pierced the floor, and if these things weren't with him, then…

"Mark, find somewhere to have a practice run first, if you insist on doing it," Vicki begged, almost in tears. That way we can time you.

"No practice runs, Vic. It'd make my legs tired, and I need them pumping. This is it. Wish me luck." He hugged and kissed all the girls in turn and took the Golden Key solemnly from King Luke. The key only just fitted in his back pocket as he forced it all the way down.

Mark put his right leg on the skateboard. He thanked his lucky stars that he had cleaned and oiled it just the other week.

And then he was off.

He pushed his right leg hard along the floor for all he was worth - once, twice, three times, four times, five times. Then his leg came up onto the board, fitting snugly into position behind the other one. He glided down the corridor at an amazing speed. Twenty yards, thirty. Then he felt himself losing momentum. He was more than two thirds of the way down the corridor, but time was running out. Again he dropped his right leg and used it to firmly build up more speed on the board, and again he rode. One second passed, two, three, four. He heard a loud metallic clunk, and was convinced that the spikes were going to pierce him and pin him to the floor. He bent forward slightly, making himself more streamlined, willing himself onto that step at the end of the corridor. He jumped from the board and landed safely. He turned, wiping sweat from his eyes and nearly sobbing with relief.

But, horror of horrors, ten feet away from him on the still-stable floor lay the Golden Key.

It must have dropped out of his pocket. It wasn't too far away, though. He leapt off the step and ran for the key without stopping to think about the consequences. If he had taken a second to think, it would have been too late, and he would never have been able to do it. He would have been stranded forever at the opposite end of the hall from the others, and the treasure would have been lost. The girls screamed, and he was dimly aware of Vicki's voice calling, "Mark, get back!"

He had reached the key, was bending to pick it up, but his head rang with the sound of screaming. He realised that one fourth of the noise was coming from him.

He had the key. He heard the rumble of the mechanism that worked the spikes. Surely, now, he would be speared before he could get back to the safety of the step. He was running. He leapt-

"KERRRRRUANK!"

-the spikes rose from beneath him even as Mark was in the air. And then he was leaning with his back against the Golden Door. Rasping breaths shuddered through his chest, which felt as though the flames of Hell were burning in it. His eyes were streaming with sweat and tears, and he could hear the girls sobbing, but it sounded as though they were a long way away. He was safe.

It took him all of two minutes to get his breath back, partly through the exertion and partly from the sheer, life-threatening terror he had just survived.

When his hands had stopped shaking, Mark put the huge key in the old-fashioned keyhole. He tried to turn it and was hit by another wave of pure, undiluted fear.

The key wouldn't turn.

After centuries of not being used, the lock had stiffened. There was no way to get back to the others, and the only way to disarm the spikes was through the door whose key wouldn't turn. Again and again Mark tried, until he was gasping in frustration.

"I can't turn it!" he shouted down the corridor.

"Keep trying!" Vicki screamed back, a note of hysteria rising in her voice.

Mark returned his attention to the lock. After several more attempts he felt the heavy key moving. He doubled his efforts until he could feel the rough golden key tearing the skin on his hands. This was, after all, a case of life or a long, slow death. Finally, the key turned, the barrel settled in the lock, and the handle twisted easily in the door.

As the door opened, shafts of sunlight spilled through the castle windows. Dust particles swam before his eyes, flitting in the light. He waited for his eyes to grow accustomed to the mottled sunlight in the golden room.

What he saw made him gasp in disbelief.

He ran to the wall to the left of the door and found the big lever that would deactivate the traps. He worried for a minute that this too would be too stiff to manoeuvre, but it moved easily in its leverage. He couldn't see the spikes retracting into the floor, but he heard them. He also heard rapid footsteps pounding down the hall towards him.

King Luke and the girls watched the spikes disappear back into the floor, and then, when it was completely safe, they set off down the corridor. At almost the same point, each of them faltered for a second: what if the mechanism was faulty and the spikes took on a life of their own and shot back up again? It didn't bear thinking about.

Vicki was the first into the treasury. She stepped over jewels and riches as though she didn't even see them and ran to hug Mark. And then the five of them stood amongst the finery, just gaping at the wonder of it all.

They were in a room the size of an average lounge. One thousand trunks of treasure had been emptied into this room. There were hundreds of thousands of golden coins, goblets and jewellery, sceptres and fine stones. There were trinkets and artefacts from the four corners of the world. The sight was simply breathtaking.

After half an hour or so, they had taken their fill of dressing in jewels and splendour, and thought it was time they were going home.

King Luke said they could each pick something from the room to take with them. It was very tempting, but how would they explain four pieces of priceless jewellery to their parents? In the end, they declined. The castle riches should stay exactly where they belonged.

King Luke had for the time being lost interest in fishing. His new love was skateboarding. Poor Mark had to leave not only his fishing rod, but also his skateboard for the young King to play with. As they were leaving, they laughed to see King Luke throwing a tantrum because he couldn't keep his balance on the board. He loved his new passtimes of 'fooshing' and 'skiteboarding' but they were going to take some getting used to. The cousins promised to return soon and hoped that he would have improved by then.

The children walked out into the Squircle. Ratchet

was screaming at Floss because she had found Kevin in her bed again. On the other side of the castle wall, they could clearly hear the gargoyles bickering…

It truly was an amazing castle.

Chapter Eleven
A New Life But Is This The End Of The Frame

'Twas the night before Christmas, and all through the house, nothing was stirring, not even a mouse. Hang on, though, Mrs Taylor *was* moving…

Debbie Taylor was moving all over the house and grumbling to anybody who would listen. It was Christmas Eve and her baby was due tonight.

"Why couldn't it have been born a week early? What kind of Christmas is this going to be? Just think, if baby doesn't come tonight I might have to be up and off right in the middle of cooking the Christmas dinner, and then where will we be? Half-cooked turkey and food poisoning all round, I shouldn't wonder. Oh, I was looking forward to a glass of wine with my Christmas lunch, doesn't look as though I'm going to get it now, though. I hope the baby waits until next week, and then at least we can get Christmas over with, and hopefully I'll be back home in time for the New Year."

Well, as it happened, baby did wait. It waited all through Christmas and Boxing Day. And then it continued to wait. In fact, it waited right through the next week. Soon it was New Year's Eve 1999. By this time, the children were thoroughly sick of waiting for their new baby. Emma and Kerry had bags packed and stacked in the hall next to Debbie's suitcase so they could be deposited at Granddad's house at a minute's notice. Every morning they all got up saying, "Today *must* be the day."

The family were very excited for other reasons, as well - a major company had offered a million pounds to the first British baby born in the new millennium. The four children, and, indeed, the rest of the family, were determined it should be theirs. All day, Debbie and her husband Steve were begging the baby not to come. "One minute after midnight, little one. That'll do nicely."

And then, as the evening arrived they were praying that it *would* come. "Come on, Fred, come on." Fred was the funny name they had given to the "bump". The children were all allowed to stay up late that night to see the birth of the new century. It was very exciting, but *something* had to be done. At ten o'clock, while the family party was in full swing at Granddad's house, Vicki called an emergency meeting. "Bedroom in five minutes," she whispered to each of the other three.

"It's ten o'clock and Auntie Debbie doesn't look as though she's going to have the baby in the next two hours," she said, once they were all together. "What are we going to do?"

Without saying a word, all four of them turned their eyes to the magic frame.

"We couldn't!" Emma gasped. "It's *so* wrong. We'd lose a berry for sure."

"Yes, but we'd still have twenty-one left. Wouldn't it be worth losing one berry *and* having a new baby in the family *and* the million pounds?"

They all sat and pondered the problem hard.

Kerry was the first to pipe up. "Sylvia would be furious," she said.

"Yes," Emma agreed. "But, what could she do about it? Once it's born she couldn't 'unborn' the baby, could she? And just think, we'd have that little baby to cuddle, and I'm sure my mum and dad would share some of the money with us. Just think what we could do with it all."

It was tempting, really, really tempting.

"What if," Vicki said thoughtfully, "what if, because we had interfered, something happened to the baby?"

They didn't like this thought one little bit and lapsed into a deep silence, each battling with their own morals and consciences.

"I vote we don't do it," Kerry said, at last. "My new brother or sister is too precious to take chances with. All in favour…?"

Instantly, there were three very firm and resolute, though somewhat reluctant, "Aye"s. It was almost with a sense of relief that they went back to join the party.

At the children's insistence - and rather against their parents' wishes - Sylvia had been invited to join the New Year's Celebrations. The children had explained to their folks that Sylvia was in fact just a lonely old lady that they had got to know quite well since the "misunderstanding" about the frame. Their parents were mistrustful of the lady who had accosted their children in the street, and it was decided that Sylvia *should* be invited so that they could get the measure of her. If need be the children would be forbidden from having anything more to do with her.

The family needn't have worried. Sylvia came

suitably dressed for the occasion, in what the children had demanded be "old granny-type" clothes. She wore a decorative scarf that hid her alarming hair, and she was sweetness itself. The children were delighted. If Sylvia became an accepted part of the "family", they would be free to visit her at Brampton Hall. Everything was going splendidly, and Nanna was very interested in Sylvia's recipe for banana bread.

When the children tried to slink back into the party, Sylvia was waiting for them at the bottom of the stairs. "Well thought through, kids. I'm proud of you, though I wouldn't have let you do it, you know."

"How did you know?" Kerry asked, shamefaced.

"Well, now, that's one of the oldest secrets of all. How did I know, indeed!" She looked left and right over her shoulder to see that nobody was listening. The children huddled in, thrilled to be on the point of discovering a new and exciting magic secret.

"Well, now, this is what I did. When you suspect four lively and headstrong children of being up to something, and you want to know what it is…," she paused.

"Yes?!" said the children, impatiently.

"Well, you follow them up to their room and listen at the door!"

"Oh, Sylvia, you are so funny!" Emma threw her arms around Sylvia's waist and hugged her hard. "We *do* love you!"

The clock struck twelve. "Auld Lang Syne" was sung with gusto, and happiness flew around the room, touching each and every one of the people present…

*

New Year's Day came and went, as did the next day, and the one after that. This was getting beyond a joke. The children were seriously beginning to doubt if the baby was *ever* going to arrive. But then, very late at night on the 4th of January 2000, two sleepy girls were dropped off at their Granddad's house and tucked straight into their beds. Very shortly after this, little Amy Taylor was born, looking surprised at her big new world and sporting a shock of jet black hair. Steve and Debbie breathed a huge sigh of relief as they gazed down on their new daughter.

Debbie was told that she had to stay in hospital with Amy for a few days to give them both a rest; coming into the world had been quite an ordeal for the new baby. The children were dying to go and see her. They hopped and jumped, begged and pleaded, but were told that they'd just have to wait for a few days to meet Amy. Steve did give Emma and Kerry a photograph of their new sister, though; it was taken in the hospital ward and showed a tiny baby with a pickled onion face and mushy-pea nose. Well, that's what Mark thought, anyway.

The next night, the four children were all staying at their grandparents' house, as it was the weekend. Sometime very late that night the plan was formulated.

"What harm would it do?" Vicki reasoned. "Everyone will be asleep. We'll just leap in, have a quick look, and then leap out again. Nobody will ever know." She was far too impatient to wait any longer to introduce herself to her new cousin. Vicki was renowned for her lack of patience. She said that, at this rate, Amy would be all grown up by the time she got to see her.

"It doesn't *sound* as though it would be wrong, but

I don't think the frame will like it. I'm not sure," Kerry said. But she wouldn't take much persuading because she too was dying to see her little sister.

Soon it was decided that they would do it. Kerry was still not sure that it was morally right. Mark was moaning that if they lost a berry not to blame him. But, really, everybody was very excited at the thought of seeing the new baby for the first time.

They put the photograph of Amy in the frame and leaped into the maternity ward at 1:05 a.m.

*

Luckily, there were no nurses in the ward and everybody seemed to be asleep. It was risky. Any of the mothers could have been feeding their babies at this time, a thought that hadn't previously occurred to them. But all was quiet. They crept down the ward, looking at the large bulges that were the sleeping mothers, and the smaller bulges in the various cots that were the sleeping babies. They stopped by Debbie's bed. The baby was wrapped in pink blankets with a little card that said, 'Baby Taylor.'

Very, very gently, Kerry pulled Amy's blanket back slightly to reveal her face. She stroked the baby's cheek with the back of her finger, and Amy moaned slightly in her sleep, but didn't stir.

Emma stood transfixed and stared at her little sister. A big tear rolled down her cheek, and Vicki put her arm round her cousin's shoulder. "Beautiful, isn't she?" Vicki said simply. Emma was so overcome with emotion that she couldn't speak, but she nodded her head in total agreement.

"Wow, chocolates," whispered Mark, staring at Mrs Taylor's bedside cabinet with widening eyes. "The babies are *great*, but just look at all those chocolates! Auntie Debbie wouldn't mind if I had just one or two." He homed in on the nearest box.

"Don't you dare," Vicki whispered. "She might wake up."

"Oh, well. We'd better be going before we get caught," Kerry said, moving away from the cot. Emma stepped forward and placed a little yellow duck that she had brought at the bottom of Amy's cot, well away from her face. Let's go," she said, wiping her cheek and leaving a big tearstain across her face.

The children joined hands and whispered the chant very quietly. Just as they were about to leap, a figure rose to an upright position in the bed opposite to the one that Debbie was in. As they left the hospital, the children just heard the start of a long, ear-splitting scream…

The scream reached the three night duty nurses in the rest room, where they were putting their feet up with a cup of coffee for a much-deserved break. They leapt from their seats and ran down the corridor to see what the commotion was. Something must have happened to one of the babies.

They hurried into the ward to find all the new mothers sitting up in bed. Several of the babies had awoken, joining in the general cacophony. Mrs Collins was sitting bolt upright in bed, screaming her head off.

"G-g-ghosts," she managed to stutter, as a nurse went to her side to try and calm her. "Four of them, children, standing right there in their nightclothes. Vanished right before my eyes, they did." The poor woman was distraught.

Sister ordered that Mrs Collins' night-time medication be changed. The sleeping pills she had been given obviously didn't agree with her.

Mrs Taylor rolled over and tried to get back to sleep. Amy had snoozed right through the incident, but would no doubt be waking up very shortly for another feed. She was a very hungry baby

"That woman is nuts," Debbie whispered to herself, looking forward to telling the family about her the next day when they visited. Strange about that little duck though, she thought. She had no idea where it had come from.

*

"Phew, that was a close one," giggled Vicki, as they had all climbed onto Mark and Kerry's beds. "I wonder what she said to the nurses?"

They chatted for a few minutes about Amy. The only reason Mark didn't tease Emma about crying when she saw her was that if the truth be known, *he'd* had to quickly wipe away a little tear himself. He was just grateful that they had all been too taken up with the baby to notice.

Plink!

"She is lovely though, isn't she?" Kerry said, "those tiny little hands, *so* perfect. Do you think she looks more like me, or more like Emma?"

Plink!

"Well, personally, I think she looks more like Gizmo the Gremlin," Emma commented. They all attacked her with pillows until she blurted out; "So cute, though! In fact, she's *adorable*."

Plink!

"Bagsee, I feed her first," Emma said.

Plink!

"What's that noise?" Mark was the first to take notice of the odd plinking that was sounding every few seconds.

They turned on the light and looked around.

Kerry gasped in horror.

The berries were falling off the frame, one by one!

The vines were withered and looked thirsty within the carved frame. The lizards were lying on their sides with their tongues lolling out of their mouths.

Plink! Another berry fell from the frame onto the mantelpiece. Vicki picked up the piece of polished wood. It turned into a desiccated berry in her fingers, all the juice and life long since sucked from it.

"I told you! I told you we shouldn't have gone to the hospital!" Kerry cried. "Now look! We haven't lost just one berry, what we did was so bad that the frame is literally dying!" Kerry burst into tears. The frame looked as though it *was* dying before their very eyes-

Plink! The last berry fell from the frame. The vines that had been so expertly carved to look alive and succulent had withered to nothing. The lizards now resembled dead lizards. The gloss was gone from their wooden eyes and the sheen had gone from their highly polished skin.

"What are we going to do? Surely, we must be able to do something?" Vicki asked no one in particular. "We can't just let the frame die."

"Let's go and see Sylvia. Maybe if we apologise she'll give us another chance," Mark suggested.

"Okay," agreed Emma. "We'll go first thing in the morning."

"*NO!*" shouted Vicki and Kerry in unison. Both of them had the same feeling of dread.

"There isn't time to wait," Vicki continued. "If we leave it until the morning, it'll be too late." She didn't know how she knew this; she just knew that something was terribly wrong and that it was true.

The children dressed hurriedly in warm clothes. After all, it *was* early January and it was freezing cold outside. They were scared as they snuck down the stairs. What if they got caught sneaking out in the middle of the night? Being up at three o'clock in the morning would take some explaining away. They could hear Granddad's loud, rumbling snore all the way down the stairs. The front door clicked loudly as they shut it behind them. They were sure it would be flung open again at any second and an angry grandparent would demand to know where they thought they were going in the middle of the night…

They didn't meet anybody on the way to Brampton Hall. In the freezing dark, everything was still and quiet.

As they let themselves in through the side gate and began the long, spooky walk up the pitch-black driveway, an owl hooted. He was annoyed to find these intruders on his hunting ground. Somewhere in the distance, his mate answered. The children drew closer together, keeping to the middle of the path so that the bony hands of the dark trees couldn't grab them and carry them away to some night-time world of horror.

Soon they were very grateful to round the last bend and see the house in sight, looming out of the darkness, nothing more than a huge black shape. Sylvia would soon be lecturing them for their foolishness and misuse of the frame, while stirring chocolate sprinkles into her excellent cocoa. Sylvia would make everything right.

"*Help me.*"

"What was that?" Mark asked, terrified. He grabbed hold of his sister in fear.

"What was what?" Vicki replied, shaking his arm loose but feeling spooked herself, nonetheless; she also thought she had heard something. "It's only the wind. Come on, we're letting our imaginations run away with us. There's nothing there."

"*Please.*"

This time there was no doubt about it. There *was* a whispering voice calling to them in the darkness. It wasn't just the below-freezing temperatures that made a chill run down their backs.

"I want to go home. I'm scared," wailed Kerry.

Something moved in the darkness. The owl swooped out of the trees, dive-bombing towards them. He flew low, furious to be disturbed in his hunt for food. Then he was gone, back into the cover of the trees, his high echoing screech ringing loud in his wake. A large shape moved on the nearby grass. They could make out its outline now.

Vicki broke from the huddle of children and started to run towards the figure lying on the frozen grass. "*Sylvia!*" She cried. "Come quick, you lot, it's Sylvia!"

They ran to their friend who was obviously in grave danger.

"Oh, thank goodness," she moaned weakly, barely able to speak. "Quick, you have to get me into the house. I'm very cold and won't last out here much longer."

Vicki took charge. Cradling Sylvia's head in her arms and making the woman as comfortable as possible, she began barking orders at the others, who, for once, were happy to be ordered about.

"Mark, go and find as many warm blankets as you can, go quickly. Kerry, go and make a cup of hot sweet tea. Emma, go to the nearest house and call an ambulance."

Sylvia didn't have a phone, because…well, because she had never known anybody who would phone her.

Lying in Vicki's arms, Sylvia had been barely conscious after having lain in the sub-zero temperatures all night. Now her eyes snapped open and her voice was drawing on all its reserves to yell, "No ambulance! I don't have mortal blood. I can't go to hospital. I need to get back to Whence, or I'll die…"

Vicki called Emma back and, instead, told her to try and find something that would help them lift Sylvia out of the snow.

Sylvia's head lolled and her eyes fluttered. The effort of talking had caused her to use the last of her strength and she was losing her fight against the darkness that was fluttering at the sides of her eyes. She was almost unconscious again, but she knew she must warn the children. In an act of sheer willpower, Sylvia opened her eyes, dispelling the night that had come to take her, driving it back with her iron-like nature. "I was coming to tell you when I tripped and fell," she said. "I've lain for hours in the snow. It might already be too late."

"Sssh, don't try to talk," Vicki said. "Just lie still."

Kat Black

Again, Sylvia raised herself up, ignoring the dizziness that was trying to take her into blessed sleep. She *had* to make the children understand the danger they were in.

"I have to tell you. You *must* listen. Adobe has been released from The Outer Whither of Whence. He is free, and he wants the frame. You must be on your guard. He doesn't know you have the frame, yet, but he will soon find out. Take care, child. I am weak, and I may not make it. I might not be here to help you."

Vicki was sobbing. "Don't say that, Sylvia. You're going to be all right. Of course, you're going to get better."

There was so much more Sylvia wanted to say, so much she wanted to warn the children about Adobe's ways, but the blackness had hold of her hand and was pulling her away with it. Her head slumped on Vicki's chest. The child was left alone in the snow with the unconscious woman. It seemed an age before the others returned.

Mark was the first back. He came with blankets and hot water bottles and they tried to make Sylvia as warm and comfortable as possible.

They tried to move the large lady onto a blanket to lift her into the house, but it was impossible, she was just *too* heavy. Her pulse was very weak. The children had no idea what her pulse should be, or even if it should be the same as a human pulse, but they did know that it shouldn't be the way it was. Sylvia was dying in the snow, and the children didn't know where to turn for help.

Kerry had been thinking. In times of trouble, Kerry did not always appear to do very much to help, but this didn't mean that her mind was inactive. "I've thought of something that might just work," she said doubtfully.

"What!" Vicki screamed at her cousin. She could feel Sylvia growing weaker and weaker beneath her. The cold had numbed Vicki through to the bone, and she was in danger of becoming hypothermic, too. Something had to be done. Anything, no matter how slim or remote a chance it was. The frame was dying because *Sylvia* was dying, not through anything they had done wrong. Surely this warning to them proved that there must be *something* they could do. They were Sylvia's last chance.

"For goodness sake, tell us!" Vicki yelled, only one step away from total hysteria. But Kerry wasn't going to be rushed. She needed to know in her mind that this was a floatable idea before she voiced it aloud. Eventually, she spoke in an agonisingly slow voice, "Vicki, I'm not at all sure what will happen, but if you go through Grandaddy into Whence, then call Sylvia in through the lizard necklace that she gave us for emergencies…wouldn't that work? Maybe?"

"Of course! Yes, that should work. Let's try it," Vicki said. "You lot stay here and look after Sylvia."

"I'll come with you, Vic, to keep you company," Mark said.

"No!" Vicki shouted at her brother, a little too sharply. He looked hurt. "No, Mark. You stay here with the others. They might need you if Sylvia gets any worse." This pacified him and made him feel important.

*

As Vicki ran through Brampton Hall, she was very aware of the danger she was putting herself in. The others had all been in the house when Sylvia had told her of Adobe's release. She was going into enemy territory without any protection, but her love of Sylvia outweighed any fears for her own safety. With a bit of luck, she wouldn't even see Adobe. She could get Sylvia the help that she needed and be back safely before anything happened. But the last thing she wanted was to put Mark at risk, too. He had almost died in the final puzzle of the castle adventure. She didn't want to take the chance of leading him into unnecessary danger again.

Before she had the chance to think about it all too much, she was in Sylvia's apartment. Granddaddy stood like a great wooden statue in the corner. He was the portal, the Way to Whence. Vicki felt a little bit scared, but she ran her hands over his big old clock face anyway:

"Granddaddy, Granddaddy, wise old Way,
Take me to Whence, please, without delay."

Within the blink of an eye, Vicki found herself in the village square of Whence. It wasn't night-time here. The sun was shining. It wasn't Wisdom Day, either, so there were no huge queues of people waiting to be given words of knowledge by the respected Olds. Nevertheless, several people went about their business, none of them giving Vicki a second glance, as though it was the most natural thing in the world for a girl from another place and time to suddenly land in the middle of their village, large as life.

Vicki put her hand to the necklace and took a deep breath before beginning the chant spell that would hopefully bring Sylvia to her:

"Sylvia, Sylvia, calling you,
I'm over in Whence, please, come on through."

Instantly, Sylvia appeared on the ground before Vicki. Her breathing was even more shallow, her skin was grey, and she seemed to be slipping away.

"Help! Help!" yelled Vicki. "I've brought Sylvia and she's very badly hurt!"

People came running from all directions. Somebody was sent to get the emergency team, someone else was sent for the Olds. People flocked around Sylvia, checking her pulse and wrapping her up.

As Vicki sat there, not knowing what to do next, Sylvia opened her rheumy eyes. "Well done, child," she croaked. "I'll be alright now. *Go,* before he gets here."

Her eyes fluttered closed again, the effort had been too much for her. Vicki bent low and kissed Sylvia's cold, leathery cheek.

"Bye, Syl. Take care, and come back soon," she whispered. She felt that Sylvia would indeed be all right, but she also felt that she would never see her special friend again. The adventures were all but finished.

Vicki stood up after leaving Sylvia in the capable hands of a large clucking woman with an ample bosom. She moved a few steps off to the left and began the chant that would take her back through Granddaddy.

"Hey, you! You there, human girl. I want to talk to you!" It was Adobe, and he was pounding towards her on his thin, bandy legs.

Granddaddy carried her, and the next thing she knew she was back in Sylvia's underground apartment. But if *she* could come through the Way, then couldn't Adobe also use the same means of travel? She felt her heart pounding. She just *knew* Adobe was right behind her, and that he was also going to burst into the flat *any second now.*

She took flight and *ran*, flinging the door open just as Adobe landed in a heap on Sylvia's polished floor. If Vicki hadn't already begun to run, he would have landed on top of her. As he leapt up to grab her Vicki slammed the door hard in his face, and then she was off, running for her life down the corridor. She could hear him in pursuit, but she dared not lose valuable time by looking behind her.

The secret door was shut. She fumbled for what seemed like an age with the lever.

He was gaining on her. "Little girl! *Dear* little girl!" he called in a thin, wheedling voice. "Any friend of my sister's is a friend of mine. Please stop and pass some time with me."

It was a trap. She didn't trust him. Instinct told her that if she stopped to talk to him, they would all be in terrible danger. This being was ruthless and he meant them no kindness.

"Little girl! My sister is asking for you, begging you to return. I heard her calling after you as you leaped."

Vicki faltered, almost stopped, almost turned to Adobe. And then, as if by magic, she heard Sylvia's voice in her mind: "Run, Vicki! Run, child! It's a trap. Do not be fooled by him. Run!" Whether this was merely her own logic, or was indeed some magic communication with Sylvia, she didn't know and didn't take the time to figure out.

She ran as she had never run before. She thought of Mark "Running the Gauntlet" on his skateboard, and she tried to capture some of her brother's courage and speed. Her legs pounded faster. And then she was in the garden hurtling at the others who were still marvelling over the disappearance of Sylvia just a few seconds before because barely any real time had passed while Vicki had been away.

"*RUN!*" Vicki screamed at them at the top of her lungs, her hair flying like a cloud of golden straw behind her. "It's Adobe! He's followed me though the Way. *RUN!*"

They could see the odd little man giving chase in the darkness. The children didn't need telling twice, they were up and off down the drive like startled rabbits.

"Don't run straight home," wheezed Vicki, "It will only lead him straight to the frame. We need to lose him first."

"*PARK!*" yelled Mark, bursting through the gates of Brampton Hall and veering off towards the equally impressive park gates at the end of the road.

Vicki was the first to tire. She had run for a considerably longer time than the others. Her breath was pounding through her body and the blood was pumping in her temples until she could feel the tune her heart was playing.

They ran straight through the park. This would not be a good place to be caught by the sinister Adobe. At this time in the morning it was still silent and deserted. When they ploughed through the park gates at the other side of the pond they split into pairs and ran in different directions, agreeing to meet back at the house when they were sure they were no longer being followed.

After flying down every back alley they could find - and giving Adobe the slip - four very tired and miserable children met up outside their grandparents' house. Quietly, they let themselves back into the house and crept silently up the stairs.

Somewhere outside, in the freezing darkness, Adobe fumed, but his anger didn't stop him feeling the cold. He soon returned to the relative warmth of Wence, via Brampton Hall...

*

Very soon, four sleepy heads hit four soft pillows. Each of the cousins grieved the loss of the magic frame in his or her own way. And that is where we leave them... for now. Because as the children slept, in a land and time far away, a lady is sitting up in bed and drinking some Lidleflower Tea. Every Whencer knows this is foul stuff, but every Whence mother also knows it is just the thing to get you on your feet again after a nasty illness.

While the children continued to sleep, the first strong shoots are breaking out from under the desiccated vines on the carved frame. Who knows, maybe these will become sweet blossom. And when the petals drop? Well, every child knows that soft sweet berries form after the fruit blossom has fallen. A whole new world awaits them while the children sleep on.